BUCK AND THE WIDOW RANCHER

When James Buckley Armstrong comes to help a recently widowed woman, somebody welcomes him with a deadly ambush. The young widow faces many problems: her husband was killed, then gambling IOUs showed up. Now a bank loan is due, and rustlers are stealing her herd. Not knowing where to start, Buck is ambushed again and beaten unconscious — and then he gets mad. Waking up with no water, no hat and no horse makes Buck ready to even the score.

CARLTON YOUNGBLOOD

BUCK AND THE WIDOW RANCHER

Complete and Unabridged

LINFORD
Leicester

First published in Great Britain in 2006 by
Robert Hale Limited
London

First Linford Edition
published 2007
by arrangement with
Robert Hale Limited
London

British Library CIP Data

Youngblood, Carlton
Buck and the widow rancher.—Large print
ed.—Linford western library
1. Cattle stealing—Fiction 2. Western stories
3. Large type books
I. Title
823.9′2 [F]

ISBN 978–1–84617–931–0

Published by
F. A. Thorpe (Publishing)
Anstey, Leicestershire

Set by Words & Graphics Ltd.
Anstey, Leicestershire
Printed and bound in Great Britain by
T. J. International Ltd., Padstow, Cornwall

This book is printed on acid-free paper

1

The big cowboy came awake instantly conscious that something wasn't right. Not moving, he looked up through the limbs of the big pine tree at the stars. Still an hour or so until the sun faded them out. Even when he got to sleep inside in a bed, as infrequent as that was, he was awake before the sun made its appearance. This time, out here in the middle of nowhere, something else had disturbed his sleep. Lying still in his bedroll he listened and heard nothing.

Until his horse blew. Not a snort, but the sharp release of air that indicated something was moving out in the darkness. The big black stud was a better watchdog than any dog could be and more than once, by a snort or a twitch of his ears, the cowboy had been warned of something he couldn't yet see or hear. Over the years, he had learned to pay attention to the big black. This time, not giving it any more thought, with his gunbelt in one hand he slipped out of the blankets and rolled silently further into the darkness of the trees. And waited.

He had found the campsite just as the sun was nearing the far mountain range. A good place with water and grass for his horse, he'd built a small fire, fixed coffee and cooked a supper of thick slices of bacon. Frying potato slices in the bacon grease and topping the meal off with a tin of peaches, the man was quite satisfied with himself and the world. Now he was trying to see if what was disturbing his horse was a danger.

Slowly, as his eyes adjusted and the stars began to grow fainter the outlines of the surrounding trees started to become more distinct. There, just about where he expected to see where he'd tied his horse on the long lead, he could make out the big black's head against the lighter background. That gave the watching man an indication of where the possible danger was coming from. Watching that area carefully, he thought he spotted some movement. Aiming his revolver at that point, he slowly and gently pulled back the hammer and waited.

Another movement in the waning darkness and he was sure; there was a man standing half hidden behind another big pine tree. Just as the weak starlight gave over to the only slightly more light of the false sunrise, the man behind the tree fired at the bedroll. Instantly two other rifles opened up, putting bullet after bullet into the twisted roll of empty blankets.

With the first shot, the hidden cowboy eased on the trigger and fired and thought he heard a grunt. Quickly he swung the long barrel in the direction of one and then the other of the attackers. A loud squeal from further out in the trees told him that a horse had been hit. Moving a few feet to the left and behind another tree, the cowboy swiftly reloaded and waited.

'Damn!' someone across the way said, his voice a weak moan. 'You've shot me. Damn.'

Except for the blubbering of the wounded horse, a quiet made more silent after the quick flurry of gunfire settled over the little glade.

For a time nothing moved. Looking toward where he'd tied the big black horse, he saw that his trusty watchdog had gone back to chomping at the grass. Whoever had been out there had left.

Waiting patiently for the sun to come up, he settled with his back against a pine and relaxed. Over in the trees he could hear the thrashing of the wounded horse. As much as he wanted to help the poor beast, he didn't trust that the wounded man wasn't still a danger. He'd wait a bit longer.

★   ★   ★

In the full of the morning's light finding the man's body was easy; he was the one who had been standing behind the pine tree and he was very dead. With that he relaxed and went to take care of the horse. A bay gelding, the animal stood some distance away with his head down and a pool of blood on the ground glistening in the morning sunshine. The bullet had gone in the animal's chest, tearing a nasty gash coming out on the other side. The blubbering he had heard was from the red froth coming from the exit wound. A lung shot. Saddened, he drew the Colt and placed the barrel against the horse's head.

'Sorry, old man,' he said quietly. 'Too bad you got caught in the mix up, but we won't let you suffer,' and he pulled the trigger.

Going through the pockets of the dead man turned up little and nothing to show his name, or why he was lying in ambush of a sleeping stranger. A small pouch with a few coins and a clasp knife with one broken blade was the sum total of the man's existence.

Taking a dirty handkerchief from the man's back pocket, Buck placed the belongings in the middle and tied the ends into a knot. Leaving the body on its back, he put the dead man's hat over his face and, after breaking camp, saddled his big black horse and rode on. He'd inform the law in town and let them take care of the body.

All he knew was three men had lain in wait for first light and then tried to kill him. Whether the idea had been to rob him or something else there was no way of knowing. Maybe someone in town would recognize the body, or the brand on the dead horse. An old brand, the scar was easy to read, the H bar H. Maybe he could learn something from that.

★   ★   ★

A little later and a few miles down the trail, the horseman sat comfortably in the saddle, listening to the late morning silence and enjoying the view of the

6

world below. Without taking his eyes off the landscape, he took a thin tobacco sack from a shirt pocket and poured a quantity of cut tobacco into a fold of paper. Still without looking to see what his supple fingers had done, he twisted the ends and, striking a wooden match on a denim-clad pants leg, put flame to the quirley.

The view that held his attention was worth taking in. From his vantage point on the rimrock above he could see the layout of the grassland below. Off to his right, a river fell in a series of cascades down to the bottomland and then flowed almost straight away far down the valley. Cattle, seen in the distance only as slow grazing brown blobs, were scattered over the near end of the basin and further out in the haze the outline of corrals and structures could just be made out. To any cattleman, this sight was a vision of heaven.

James Buckley Armstrong, called by those who knew him simply as Buck, was a cattleman, born and bred. A cattleman, he smiled at the thought, without even one head to call his own. He was, he realized a long time ago, a happy cattleman because without the troubles and tribulations that owning land or cattle brought, he was able to see life as simply one adventure after another. A big man, even sitting astride his horse, anyone could see he was bigger than average. Standing slightly over six feet tall in his stockinged feet, when he could afford stockings, his erect posture in the saddle made it obvious that somewhere in his thirty years there had been military training. In the course of his adult years he'd traveled far and had done many things, many of which involved using what he'd learned while wearing a uniform. Now, in his trail-worn denim pants, faded red shirt and scarred boots with rundown heels, it was clear he was a cattleman.

Still with a smile lighting his face he finished his smoke and taking a last long look at the valley below, nudged his black horse with the blunt end of a spur and headed on down the trail. Coming into the valley by this back country route rather than along the stage line was no accident. His plan was to arrive unnoticed and unknown. Now, with a dead man back there, that might not be possible. The trail was not a well-used track and from the lack of fresh horse prints, not used often. Taking his time and moving carefully, Buck held his horse back.

'There ain't much of a reason to go barreling down this hill, horse,' he told the stallion. 'Let's plan on getting to the bottom without busting a leg, yours or mine,' Buck said in a quiet voice. Long used to hearing comments from the man on his back, the big black stallion didn't even acknowledge the words by so much as a twitch of its ears. The horse was not a great beauty, hard-mouthed, strong-willed and pigheaded with what appeared to be a bad temper and able to show only a tolerant respect for the man on his back. The two had been partners for a long time, though, and were rarely far from each other.

Once on the more level plain, and still not in any hurry, Buck took his time riding along the fast-moving river, stopping every so often to inspect the deep slower moving pools at the head of stretches of rapids. This, he decided, would be a good place to come back to for a spot of fishing. Lazing in the morning sun, he tried to remember the last time he'd had the time to simply spend fishing and daydreaming. Far too long, he concluded. Well, maybe this is the time to change that . . . once he took care of whatever the Professor had asked him to do.

With a final shake of his head, he turned his back on the rushing water and directed his big black mount out into the wild grass-covered prairie. There, nudging the horse into a distance-eating canter, he started passing small bunches of cattle. The mounted rider offered no danger to these grazing herds and only when he got too close did any even notice his existence. Other than the sound of his horse's hoofs hitting the grass, the day remained nearly as quiet as when he was back up on the rim. Relaxed in the saddle, Buck soon reached the well-maintained outbuildings of a working cattle ranch. Slowing at the corner of a large pole corral, he sat his horse for a moment and looked over the big house, barns, bunkhouse and other smaller structures.

A fly-screen-covered door in one of the smaller buildings close to one end of the veranda flew open and a pan of water was thrown out. This, he decided, would be the cookhouse. Other than that quick movement and the flicking tails of a pair of horses that stood hipshot at a hitch rail in front of the veranda that ran the entire length of the house, nothing moved. After taking in the peaceful scene, Buck nudged his horse with a heel and rode across to the hitching rail.

He was about halfway across the empty yard when the front door opened and two men walked across the porch followed by a slightly built woman. Seeing the horseman all three stopped and stared. Reaching up slowly with his left hand, Buck tipped his hat.

'Afternoon, ma'am,' he smiled, and looking the two men over, nodded.

'You see, Matilda?' the bigger of the two said, not taking his eyes off the mounted man. 'This is just what I was talking about. Here's a day when all your hands are out on the ranch and in comes a stranger. You can never know what might happen. You,' he raised his voice and called to Buck. 'What might you want, creeping up like that?'

It was easy to see the two men were related. Both were wearing the same type of working clothes, black denim pants tucked into shotgun boots. Worn boots that made clear neither were wearing their Sunday-go-to-meeting out-fits. Tall, both were close to Buck's six feet but he'd guess that the younger of the two was a little heavier, his body carrying a little more weight with the extra looking soft. Clean-shaven, the older man's mustaches reached below the ends of his mouth. Neither man looked happy, but from where he was sitting, Buck guessed that happiness was uncommon with them.

Buck's smile, if anything, got wider but he didn't respond to the question. After reaching up to touch his hat he had let his left hand fall naturally to rest on the saddle horn. His right hand was hanging easily from his thumb that was stuck in his wide leather gunbelt just inches from the butt of his .44 Colt Dragoon. Buck had already taken in the gunbelts on the two, what looked to be a Colt Peacemaker on the young man's hip, an older revolver holstered on the other.

'Hugh, this is nothing for you to question about. Remember, this is my ranch and I'll decide if this rider is my guest or what. And I'll have you know I am not alone. If you'll get off your high horse and look over there, you'll see that Cookie and his helper are there if needed.' All three men glanced in the direction of the woman's nod to find two men, one no more than a boy, facing them, both with double-barreled guns. From that angle it was clear that the woman would be the only one standing if a trigger was pulled.

'Don't mean no harm, ma'am,' Buck said, moving his right hand to cover his left on the saddle horn. 'Certainly not with half an army facing me.'

'Damn it, Matilda, it just ain't safe you being here by yourself. I'm only trying to do the neighborly thing and make sure you're not in harm's way.'

'Hugh, I grew up on this ranch and with Cookie and Freddie looking out for me, I am safe. Thank you for worrying, but I can take care of myself.'

The man, after returning his look at Buck, motioned for the other to follow and untied his horse. 'All right, I see you're going to be stubborn. Just remember, I'm there if you need me. And think about what I said inside. The sign is clear; you've been losing cattle.

You can't run a place this size by yourself and, well, I'm there for you. C'mon, Frank,' he said, reining his horse around, touching a spur to the animal and leading the other man out of the ranch yard at a gallop.

The woman watched them go and then turned to study Buck. After a minute she turned back to the pair of guards. 'It's OK, Cookie, Freddie. This is the man I told you about. Thank you for being ready, though. I do believe Mr Hightower thinks too much of himself and your being here helped take a bit of wind out of his hat.' The last said with a little chuckle.

'Welcome,' she went on, motioning him to tie up at the rail. 'Come on in and have a cup of coffee. The pot is fresh made.'

2

Before dropping the reins over the hitch rail, Buck led his horse to a nearby water trough and let him drink. Matilda watched.

A few minutes later, seated comfortably around the big kitchen table, she smiled. 'I would hazard a guess that you're the friend Uncle Fish told me to look out for,' she allowed, pouring him a mug of black strong-looking coffee. 'There was a letter from him telling me to watch out for a big, rangy man riding a big black horse that looks even rougher. That'd be you. My name is Matilda Randle.'

'Yep,' Buck smiled, and introduced himself.

Following her into the house, he had been led through the front room down a short hall and into a sun-washed kitchen. The big room at the front, with its huge stuffed buffalo head mounted over a rock fireplace, each of the river-smoothed stones being bigger than a man's head, was clearly a man's room. This was a comfortable room full of worn oversized leather and polished wood furniture. The kitchen, on the other hand, was a woman's domain.

A large black Peninsular woodstove, its silver trim around the fire box and big oven gleaming in the sunlight, took up nearly all one wall. A stone dry sink and thick plank-topped work counter lined another. Windows, each with bright yellow and white curtains, framed the windows on three walls, letting the bright late morning sunshine fill the room. Seated at the table that was big enough to sit six or eight comfortably, Buck blew some of the steam off the cup and watched the woman as she returned the big fire-blackened pot to the back of the stove.

A young woman, he judged, probably five years or so younger than he was.

Somewhere in her mid to late twenties, he'd say. A proud woman, one who would not take lightly to being ordered around by any man, unless he was her man. A ranch woman, she was probably a strong and capable person, he thought. The kind of woman that, having grown up on a ranch, was able to handle herself well and not faint away at the first hint of trouble. Just the kind of woman, he said to himself, that he would marry. But then, he completed the thought: he just wasn't the marrying kind.

Buck watched her, noting the smoothness of the dress over her upper body. He didn't know much about dresses and dress material, but had noticed time and again how some women seemed to fill out a dress better than others. This dress, at least to the point just below her waist where the bottom flared out, fitted this woman's body as if it had been sewn on. A wonderful sight, he thought, all smooth and full of curves. Shoulder-length hair, light brown and wavy, was held in place by a wide band of ribbon. Her eyes were of a light blue color that was almost the pale shade of the sky just before sundown.

'Tell me, how well do you know Professor Fish?' Buck leaned back in the big chair, deciding it was best not to look too far into her eyes or he might get lost.

'I know him as Uncle Fish. And I've known him pretty much all my life,' she smiled.

'Uncle Fish? That's a new one on me. I've only ever heard him called the Professor or Professor Fish. Is he your uncle?'

'He was almost my father,' she answered, laughing. 'I grew up knowing him. He and my father were great friends and at one time both the men courted my mother. Father won out, and Uncle Fish stayed around, helping turn this end of the valley into the Rocking C. He was here until I was at least ten years old. I think he stayed around just in case my mother ever changed her mind. He really isn't my uncle, you know, but he's about the closest thing I have to any relatives. My husband Virgil was an orphan, so there's just been him and me.'

'Do tell. I've known the Professor for ten years or so and somehow I just can't see him courting a woman. But yes, I did get a letter from him asking if I was to ride in this direction would I stop by and see what kind of trouble was coming your way.'

'I didn't know what else to do, or who else to turn to when Virg was shot. The town sheriff wouldn't even come out when I reported it. He said anything outside the town limits was outside his jurisdiction.'

'And there isn't a marshal in this area?'

'No. I didn't know what to do. Nobody seemed to care that my husband had been killed. For a while I was knocked for a loop. Hugh came over a couple times to help out, and Hank, our foreman, and the hands, well they really took care of things. Kept everything running the way it should.'

'Tell me about your husband's shooting.'

'I don't know much. When he didn't come in from a trip to town, Hank took a couple of the boys and rode back that way to see if Virg'd had some trouble with the wagon. He'd been in picking up supplies and was due back by dark. It's a good two or three hours or so into town and he didn't like being on the road after dark with the wagon. They found him on the other side of the river. He'd been shot in the side and was lying in the dirt next to the road. The wagon and all the supplies was just standing there. Hank used his bedroll and wrapped Virg up and brought him home in the back of the wagon.'

'And the sheriff didn't come out to even look at the body?'

'No. I sent Hank in, but Sheriff Holt said there was nothing he could do. We buried Virgil up alongside Pa's grave. Up on a little hill overlooking the ranch yard. We'd only been married six years.'

'Your letter didn't say much about the kind of trouble you were having, at least the Professor's letter to me didn't. You have any idea who would shoot your husband?'

'I don't know. All I do know is that a few days after we talked to the sheriff I had a visit from a well-dressed man I'd never seen before. He said his name was Vance Hubbard and he was holding a couple IOUs for debts my husband had owed. That was the first I heard of that. Virg had never said anything about owing anyone money.'

'Did the Hubbard fellow say what that debt was for?'

'Yes. He said it was a gambling debt. He claimed Virgil had lost in a poker game and didn't have enough money to cover his losses. Virgil never played poker that I knew of.' She stopped and brushed at her cheek. 'I'm sorry,' she said, getting up to get the coffee pot.

'That's OK. A person has a right to mourn for a loved one and I don't think there's a time limit on how long that mourning can last. Probably as long as it has to, I'd say.'

'The thing that makes me mad,' she said, filling both Buck's cup and her own, 'is that I'm not sure whether I'm crying over losing Virgil, or because I'm so damn mad that no one would do anything to find out who shot him.'

Buck sipped at the hot coffee and let a few minutes pass before asking her what kind of man her husband had been.

'He was a good man, well educated, but for all that still good at making this ranch profitable. Anyway, he worked hard and had some plans for expanding the irrigation ditches my pa had put in. There's a lot of land over to the east that would produce better beef if we could get more water to it. Virgil wanted to upgrade the kind of beef we raise, too. Get in a couple of white-face Herefords.'

'Tell me about this ranch and the surrounding country.'

'Well, the Rocking C property runs from about halfway up that hillside back there by the falls and then all along the rimrock to the east. The boundary to the west is the river and the southern end is where the river bends around and crosses the valley. There is a bridge across the river there that my father, Jim Coulter, had built a few years before he died. The town, Coulter's Landing, was named after him. It's about five miles on down the road from our boundary.'

'What's on the other side of the river up here?'

'The Hightower place. Hugh Hightower's the man who was here when you rode in. The other man was Frank, Hugh's oldest son. He has three sons and they run horses over there. His land is long and narrow. Just as this ranch, it starts up at the foothills and is bordered by the rimrock on one side and the river on the other. His place runs further south than this, though.'

'And what's down below the river?'

'There're a handful of small spreads. Squatters, Hugh calls them. There are a couple of pretty good sized farms down there and below town on both sides of the river. A few Basque sheepherders run their flocks in the dry country to the east. Away from the river it gets pretty dry and that makes it just about right for sheep. Beyond there's a long wide stretch of sand blow. No water until you get across to the Red River. A lot of people have died trying to ride across without carrying enough water.

'Anyway, Pa was the first one in the valley. The Hightowers came in a few years later and took up their land, Hugh and his first wife, Kathleen, and the two oldest boys. We were all good friends then. I remember growing up and having Kathleen Hightower and her boys, Frank and Hughie coming over to visit my ma every so often. We'd play all day in the barn or riding our ponies. Then Ma died, caught the flux, the town doctor said. It wasn't but a year or so after that Kathleen passed away. A while later Hugh remarried and his third son was born. I don't remember her name. I never met her. She died when the boy came. His name is Paul.

'Pa said that having the farmers taking up land south of town helped make the valley strong. Hugh didn't agree. I remember he always said that land should be used for raising livestock. Putting a plow to the ground was destroying it, he claimed. Pa only laughed and said he had enough and someone else could use the rest. Until my husband was killed this valley was a wonderful place to live.'

'What did your Mr Hightower mean about you missing some cattle?'

'I don't know. Hugh came by a few days ago saying his son Frank was coming back from a horse-buying trip and found sign over along the east wall of a couple small bunches being pushed south. We decided to start gathering a herd of older stuff for a drive later to the railhead. That's where the hands are now, out pushing everything into a holding ground. We'll pick out the young stuff to keep over the winter and sell off the older beeves. I asked Hank to take a look and let me know. He won't be back to the ranch for another two or three days.'

Buck finished his coffee and pushed away from the table. 'Well, I don't know what I can do to help, but I can start by checking out those IOUs and maybe stop in and talk with the sheriff.'

Picking up his hat, she followed him back out to the front porch. For a few minutes they stood looking out over the spread, taking in the late afternoon silence. Other than the soft clucking coming from a chicken coop somewhere out of sight and the random call of a calf for his mama, the place was peacefully quiet.

'Why are you doing this?' she enquired. 'Are you here just because Uncle Fish asked you to be?'

'Yeah. I owe the Professor a lot, a lot more than I can ever repay, to tell the truth. And then I didn't have any reason to be where I was at the time, so when I got his letter, well, I guess it gave me a direction to ride. A new place to see and new people to meet.'

'Don't think I'm not grateful, but I just want to know what you're getting out of it. Hugh thinks you and every other man is just trying to move in on the ranch and me. If he had his way I'd become his third wife,' she smiled. 'But that's not likely. Why, I'm only a little older than his oldest son. He's almost as old as my pa was. No, it's not likely. But he does think I need protecting. You should know that.'

3

Matilda suggested that she fix an early supper and then she'd ride in with Buck. Tired of his own cooking, which usually meant something cooked over an open fire, and then, five out of six times being burnt, he quickly agreed. Shooed out of the kitchen, he found comfort in one of the rocking chairs on the front porch and rolled a smoke.

★ ★ ★

The ride into town was a pure delight for Buck. After pinching out his cigarette and before being called in to the meal, he'd gone down to the creek that ran behind the barn and, finding the pool, stripped out of his dusty clothes and soaked for a few minutes in the cold water. Clean and refreshed with a shave, and with a clean shirt, he felt pretty good. Supper was another enjoyable time. Matilda had poured him a glass of amber-colored whiskey that went down so smooth he wondered how the liquid could be contained in the bottle. After the meal, made even better by having such an attractive woman on the other side of the table, they sat for a time on the front porch. Buck savoring another shot of the liquor with a hand-rolled cigarette.

After saddling a dun-colored horse for Matilda and tightening the cinches on his own saddle, they rode away from the ranch. As they slowly rode south, the ranch-owner pointed out various aspects of the property — where her father had fenced off a section and dug the irrigation ditches to take water to a large garden, and later the bridge over the river.

'This is my property line,' she said. Then pointing to a rutted wagon road angling off to the west, she explained that was the edge of the Hightower ranch. 'Hugh was younger than my pa when they came into the valley. Pa got here a little before him and had marked out the boundaries he wanted. Hugh looked the rest of the basin over and decided, rather than take up land south of the river, he would take the western strip. It's a lot less land that he could've had, but he told Pa it would be better for raising horses. Guess he knew what he was talking about. He and his boys work hard, and they've got a good spread.'

After crossing the river, talk between them died out until they reached the outer edges of town. Typical of small towns throughout the state, Coulter's Landing was no more than a dozen or so buildings, mostly flat-roofed, single-storey clap-board structures with only a handful having a second floor. The hotel was the tallest building, boasting three levels. Off behind the shops and businesses Buck could see a number of shanties and pole and sod dwellings. The residential side of town, he thought.

A curtain-sided stagecoach pulled by a six-horse hitch was just coming into town as they rode past the first few buildings. Matilda pointed to the tallest structure. 'The stage is the town's link to the railroad station at Brisby,' she said. 'Comes into town in the evening and leaves in the morning. I'll stop off and leave my grocery list with Mr Lathrop at the store,' she said, pointing toward one of the buildings, 'and meet you later at the restaurant. We can have a cup of coffee before we head back.'

'I guess finding the sheriff's office won't be hard. If I get lost I can always find my way back here and ask directions.' Laughing, he tipped his hat and rode at a walk on down the street.

Wide enough for a pair of stage-coaches to pass each other, the street was probably either a frozen washboard in winter or a mud-choked swamp, depending on the severity of the weather. Now with summer about half over the thoroughfare was hock deep in dust. Every step his horse took sent up little puffs of the fine-ground soil. On either side, rough plank walkways ran along the fronts of the various stores and shops. Most of these were shaded by sun-blocking wood plank or canvas awnings from which signs announcing the kinds of product one could buy hung over the walkways. Finding the sheriff's office was made easy by the big, five-pointed sign hanging above the door to that building. Tying his horse next to others at the rail in front, Buck settled his heavy gunbelt around his hips and pushed through the office door.

Two men sitting on either side of a big dark-wood desk had been talking but fell silent as he came in out of the afternoon sun. Letting his eyes adjust to the murkiness of the room, Buck noted the shiny star badge pinned to the man sitting behind the desk before taking in the other man. Big like a cloud is big just before letting go with a rain squall, the man's small, close-spaced eyes were centered in the middle of a round, smooth face. Those black eyes stared back as Buck took in the Coulter Landing's elected lawman. The pointed star was pinned to the pocket of a shirt that had once been white but since being washed at the laundry had taken on a dingy gray color. A sagging pot belly hung over the waist of a pair of dark pin-striped wool pants, which were held in place by a pair of black suspenders.

'Well, stranger? Are you going to waste our time staring or have you got some business here . . . law business,' the sheriff said almost angrily. 'You barged in on a private conversation, you know.'

Nodding his apologies, Buck turned back toward the door. 'Sorry about that. Tell you what, I'll go have a cup of coffee at the hotel and once you've finished with your private business and want to do some public law business, you come on over. I'll buy you a cup, Sheriff.'

'No,' the older of the two men said,

rising from his chair. Shorter and only coming up to Buck's shoulder as he stood, this man was obviously not a rancher. A heavy gold chain hung across his vest from a buttonhole across to a slit pocket. The vest, suit coat and pants all were well-pressed gray wool. Flat-heeled leather shoes covered the man's feet, feet that were tiny in relation to the rest of his body. 'That won't be necessary, young man. My business with Sheriff Holt will wait.'

'What kind of story you got to share with us, cowboy?' Buck decided he didn't like the sheriff's attitude and wouldn't vote for him any time in the near future.

'My name is James Buckley Armstrong and I'm here to tell you about a body that's needing burial.'

'What body?' the rotund sheriff asked, standing up and reaching for a light-colored Stetson hanging on a hook. 'Where is it?'

'Out north of Mrs Randle's spread. You'll find him lying in a stand of big pine trees right near a little creek, just off the trail a bit. I hung a bit of cloth on a limb to mark the spot.' Buck stopped as the sheriff put the hat back on the peg and sat back down.

'Anything out of town is out of my jurisdiction, cowboy,' he said. 'Do you know who the man is?'

'Nope. No identification in his pockets. Fact is,' Buck said, placing the previous owner's belongings still wrapped in the kerchief on the desk, 'this is all he had in his pockets.'

The sheriff untied the knots and looked through the dead man's belongings. Shaking his head, he looked at the other man, 'Any idea who this belonged to, Mr Blount?'

The other man leaned over and, using a finger, poked the meager possessions before shaking his head.

'Well, that doesn't tell us much, stranger. How did this man die, anyhow?'

'I shot him,' Buck allowed. 'There's a dead horse nearby. I'd say it was my bullet that caused his death, too.'

Scowling, the lawman stared up at Buck. 'Mind telling us how you came about shooting this man and his horse?'

'I'm not sure it was his horse. There were at least three men and I only found one body and one horse. The horse had a brand that you might recognize, looked like a H Bar H.'

'That'd be one of Hightower's horses. Hell, everybody rides a Hightower horse. You say there were at least three men? When was this?'

'Daybreak. From the way they shot up my blankets, I'd say they were trying to stop my snoring . . . permanently. They made too much noise sneaking up in the dark and when they opened fire I was ready. Surprised them, I'd say. I hit one and the others took off.'

'And you didn't see anyone you could describe? Now, why would three strangers want to shoot you up? Could there be someone coming after you?'

'Doubt it. I don't know too many people in this part of the country.'

'May I enquire as to what your business is in this area?' asked Blount, breaking his silence. 'None of my business, I know, but, well, when a stranger comes in to report having killed a man, it does make one wonder.'

'Yep. Makes me wonder why a bunch of hardcases would want to put holes in me, too. My business here? Just stopping off to look up a friend of a friend. As I said, my business.'

'And who,' Sheriff Holt asked, still watching Buck's face closely, 'could that friend of a friend be?'

'Why, Mrs Randle, Sheriff. Seems she has had some trouble. Her husband shot just outside of town and all. Too bad you didn't look into that murder, though. Might have saved my riding over and nearly getting killed myself.'

'Ah, the Widow Randle,' Blount murmured softly. 'Are you close to the young lady?'

'Close enough, I'd say. What's your interest in her?'

'I'm the banker and my interest with

her is, I'm afraid, between she and I.'

'And, I'd guess, the sheriff. Well, I'm on my way to meet her. Care to come along? I'll even buy you a cup of coffee,' suggested Buck.

'Um, yes,' the banker said, nodding. 'Now might be a good time to talk with her. Sheriff Holt, thank you for your time and good day.' Putting a short-brimmed hat squarely on his head the banker reached for the door knob. Buck, standing to one side of it, had his hand on it first and opened it for the other man.

'Stranger,' Sheriff Holt said with authority, 'I'm not sure we're through talking about that man you killed.'

'Why, Sheriff, it happened far outside the town limits. Of course, I understand how busy you must be just keeping the peace in this fine city. I guess the next thing for me to do is to contact the governor's office and request that a marshal be sent in to investigate both that shooting and Randle's murder. I gather you haven't done that, have you?'

Buck watched as he spoke and saw a small tightening of Holt's eyes. Then, once again smiling, the sheriff nodded. 'Of course, that is the right thing to do. But, stranger, I trust you'll remain in the area in case there are any questions? Seems strange to me, your coming in just about the time that poor Mrs Randle is having all her trouble.'

'Yeah, I don't have any place I'd rather be. What with a report of some rustling at the Rocking C and all, I guess I'll stick around.' With one hand on the smooth handle of his Colt six-gun Buck smiled at the rotund officer of the law. 'Don't forget, Sheriff, your jurisdiction ends at the edge of town. You don't want to get involved with anything outside your range, now do you?'

'No, you're right, of course. Forget I said anything.'

Nodding to the man, Buck pushed through the door and out into the sunshine.

Coming into the restaurant, he saw that the banker had just reached Matilda's table. He was pulling out a chair when Buck walked up and, smiling at the young woman, took a chair on the other side of the table.

'Huh, Mrs Randle,' Blount said, frowning in Buck's direction, 'this business might be better discussed privately.'

'Mr Blount, I believe anything you have to tell me can be said in front of my friend Mr Armstrong,' Matilda answered.

'Well, if you insist.' Obviously the banker wasn't happy with it, but went on, 'I am very sorry about the death of your husband and hope you accept my condolences. However, even with such a terrible thing happening, business must go on. It pains me to trouble you with this, but the due date on your note is just a week away.'

'My note? What note would that be, Mr Blount?'

'To be clear, it is a note the bank holds signed by your late husband. According to the law, with his death that becomes the obligation of the next of kin, and that, I'm afraid, is you.' Sincerity seemed to seep from the banker as he explained, hands held out with palms up and his smile appearing gentle and sad. Buck smiled at Matilda.

'How much is this note for and when did Virgil take out this loan?' he asked.

'Stranger,' — the sound of sincerity was gone, replaced by a mixture of anger and authority — a banker's voice — 'this matter is between Mrs Randle and the bank. You have no place in this.'

'Mr Blount,' Matilda asked gently and with a great smile, 'How much is this note for and when did Virgil take out this loan?'

Buck smiled at the growing frown on the banker's face. 'About two weeks before his untimely death, Virgil came into the bank and took out a loan for twelve hundred dollars which he said was to be used to purchase a Hereford bull. Under the terms of that loan, the amount plus interest is to be paid off in monthly instalments with the first payment due and payable in seven days from today.' Finished, Blount settled back in his chair, keeping his eyes on Matilda, not even glancing in Buck's direction.

Matilda looked down at the table for a few minutes and then taking a sip of coffee from her cup, looked back across the table. 'Thank you, Mr Blount, for bringing this to my attention. Now, if you'll excuse us?'

That wasn't what he had expected, it was clear. Glaring at Buck, the banker stood and nodding to Matilda walked out of the restaurant.

'Buck? What is happening? Virg wouldn't do something like that without our talking it over. We discussed everything and the purchase of a bull wasn't in the plans until next spring.'

'I don't know. It seems that someone is trying to dump a big load on you. There's that gambler trying to call a gambling debt, some rustling and now a bank note. And all this coming at you since your husband was murdered and left by the side of the road. I don't know what I can do, but maybe it is time to send a letter to the governor's office.'

4

Getting back to the ranch just as darkness came on, Buck joined Matilda in the cook shack for a late dinner of steak, potatoes, and snap beans, topped off with a big piece of apple pie. All washed down with cups of coffee from the jug the cook's helper never let get empty.

Spreading his bedroll on one of the empty bunks in the bunkhouse, Buck spent a full night without being shot or having a rock or stick poke him in the back. Up before the sun peeked over the far rimrock, he was pleasantly surprised to find that Freddie had already made coffee. Before finishing his first cup of the strong black brew, a plate covered with slices of ham, eggs and thick slices of bread was put before him.

The big black stud horse had heard

him coming and was waiting at the corral gate when Buck, carrying his saddle and gear, got there. Within minutes, and after telling the cook's helper to tell Matilda that he'd be back in a day or two, he was riding. Maybe there wasn't much he could do about a gambling debt or a bank loan, but seeing about rustlers seemed like a good idea.

* * *

Finding the ranch crew and making sure they knew what he was doing on the property seemed like another good idea, but not one easily done. Matilda had never mentioned exactly how big the ranch was and probably didn't know. From the river west to the rimrock, from the bridge to the south and again to the foothills on the north didn't suggest how many acres. Shortly before the sun reached its highest peak for the day Buck had found out for himself just how big the Rocking C was; from every high place he could find all he could see was more ranch. It was a thin wisp of smoke that led him to the crew.

Riding closer to the smoke he started coming upon more and more beeves. All during his ride he had seen small bunches of nondescript cattle here and there but as he neared where the men were working the numbers increased. Finally from the top of a small rise he could see what was happening. The smoke came from a pair of fires in which the handles of a dozen or so branding irons stuck out. As a rider roped a calf or yearling from the herd and dragged him toward the fires, another man, on foot and wearing leather gloves, would take an iron and burn the brand into the squalling beef. If a bull, another man would step in and in one quick swipe castrate the animal, smearing the wound with a dab of sticky black substance. Once released the calf would rush back to find his mother and the pair would find

47

themselves herded out of the bunch and left to wander off.

Other riders circled the herd and in turn sent their loop over the next young animal to be branded. Still others could be seen in the distance herding small gatherings toward the holding herd. As Buck watched he had to nod in appreciation at the organization he saw. Whoever was in charge was doing a good job of getting the most out of his men without overworking anyone. A movement to his left caught his eye and looking he saw a horseman coming his way. He was, he figured, about to meet Hank the foreman.

'Morning,' Buck said as the other rode in. Tilting his hat back on his head, Buck had placed both hands on his saddle horn. 'Just appreciating the work going on down there and glad I'm not part of it.'

'They're a good bunch of hands,' the foreman allowed. 'Anything in particular we can do for you?'

'Well, maybe. I'm Buck Armstrong.

Out here looking things over for Mrs Randle. She tells me you found some sign recently that made you wonder about rustlers.'

Hank slowly took in the big man and his mount. Nodding he smiled. 'Yeah, I figured it'd be you. Miz Randle told me you'd be coming around sooner or later and I gotta tell you, I'm glad it's sooner. She's got enough on her plate to have to worry about some curly wolf cow-thieves.' Sticking his big rope-scarred hand out, he added, 'I'm the foreman, Hank Bowers.'

Taking the hand, Buck asked about the possibility of cattle rustlers working the area.

'Naw, we haven't lost any head in a long time. Fact is I can't recall ever losing any. Oh, the odd cow'll be cut out and run off. I figure that's just some sodbuster from down south putting in a bit of winter eating. But this time, well, I think it was more than that. Probably some thirty or forty head.'

'Any idea of how many riders were

doing the job?' Buck pulled the makings from a shirt pocket and, after offering the sack to the foreman, rolled a quirley.

'Maybe half-a-dozen riders,' Hank answered, shaking out the tobacco into the thin paper and rolling his own smoke. 'It was on south of here, over near where the bluff peters out. That rimrock just fades away the further south you go. South of the property a ways it almost melts into flat land. A lot of dry land farming down there. The herd looked to be pushed south, but I doubt if any of the farmers down there saw them. I expect they were headed out into the flats and around. Go south far enough and you come to the Big Valley railhead. That's where all the ranches in this area and those further down the valley ship their livestock from.'

Watching the hands work the herd below, Buck asked, 'Exactly where did you find the sign?'

'East of here and a little south. When

you get close to the rim watch for a big tall slab-sided rock sticking straight up. It goes up a couple hundred feet, I'd guess. Some dude once explained that way back when, that was the inside of a small volcano. I don't understand it exactly, but the story is that over the centuries the volcano cooled and the mountain around the hard rock weathered away, leaving that finger sticking up. I dunno about that, but we use that landmark as the southern boundary.

'Anyway, just a bit south of there, close to where the land slopes up is where we found the trace. It was a couple of days old to look at it so we didn't follow it. Maybe should have, but we were starting this gather and had other things to worry about.'

Buck carefully put his cigarette out and, settling his hat squarely on his head, thanked the foreman. 'Well, I don't know what I'll find now, but guess I'll go take a look. Thanks for your help, Hank. I'll probably see you back at the ranch, sooner or later.'

'Oh, one other thing. There's a couple of sheepherders that run their flocks down there. Just to let you know. Maybe they saw something, if you should happen across them.'

Reining the black away, Buck nodded and headed south.

★　★　★

It was much later in the afternoon when Buck found a small spring and watered his horse. Hoofprints, not only cattle, but that of deer and other wildlife had led him to the spring that was hidden behind a thick growth of brush. Only the bushes close to the water were green, the outer layer sunbaked and brown. Anyone missing the animal tracks could very easily have ridden on by and never known there was water there.

Riding on he sighted the towering rock finger and even from a distance could tell it was a good marker. Straight and slick-sided, it was as Hank said, very identifiable.

Again it was the smoke that gave him direction. Making his way around the base of the monolith Buck came upon a herd of woollies. The smoke was pouring out of a tin chimney pipe sticking at an angle out the side of a canvas-covered wagon. Stopping well away from the wagon, Buck raised one hand and yelled out, 'Hello the wagon.'

A door, unseen from where he sat, opened in the back of the wagon and an older man stepped down. After taking a minute to inspect the visitor, the man waved Buck in.

'Welcome, stranger. Welcome to my fire. It is good for you to arrive now as we can be hospitable and invite you to share our supper.' The man was, Buck saw as he climbed down from the saddle, older than he first thought. Wrinkles lined his sunbrowned face and under a narrow-brimmed floppy hat, hair that had once been black was streaked with gray and hung down to his shoulders in uncut strands. Sharp black eyes watched as the horseman loosened the saddle cinches and removed the bridle bit. Looping the reins over the saddle horn, Buck let the big black search out the few tufts of dried grass missed by the sheep. Too close to the wagon, he thought.

The sheep, some standing, most lying about in a huge cluster, had not shown any fear or excitement on the rider's approach. Buck didn't know much about sheep, but the Professor had once explained that most cattlemen were wrong, the two herds could live in close proximity to each other.

'My son will be joining us soon,' the older man said. Then, pointing to his chest, he added 'My name is Juan Navarro and this is my flock. They have had a good day of grazing and will now rest and be ready for what tomorrow brings. Here,' he went on, motioning to Buck, 'get comfortable and I will bring the coffee pot from the wagon.'

Finding as soft a spot as he could, Buck had no more than settled down when the grizzled old man came out with an enameled pot and three off-white mugs.

'My son will be along in a few minutes. I am sure he will be glad to see we have a guest for dinner. Following the flock often gets lonely and a guest is a wonderful way to end a beautiful day, wouldn't you say?' His speech was almost without accent but something made Buck realize he was a foreigner.

Almost as if he had read the big cowboy's mind, Juan Navarro explained, 'We are Basque. Herding and caring for sheep is a long tradition in our country. My son is part of the old country and part of this new land. The customs are different and caring for the flock is too often a lonely time. My son will enjoy your company as he is not used to being without people around him.'

Buck relaxed with the cup of fireside coffee but when his horse's head came up and turned to look off to one side, he noticed. Moving slightly and adjusting his holstered six-gun, the big cowboy was watching as a second man came striding through the brush and into camp, a lamb tucked under one arm. It was obvious these two men were related. The younger man stood straight where his father's shoulders were slightly stooped. Where the older man's hair was mostly gray-streaked, his son's was shiny black. Both were weeks from the barber's shears. However the chief difference, Buck was quick to notice, was that while the father was friendly and welcoming the son was not.

'Who are you?' he greeted Buck, stopping and standing straight and stiff.

Before he could respond, Juan Navarro chastized his son. 'He is a guest in our camp, Jose, and will be treated with respect.' Gone was the soft melodious voice.

'Father, you don't know what you leave yourself open to, letting just anyone come in.' Keeping one eye on Buck, he bent over and released the lamb who, with a bleat, scrambled away and was instantly lost in the flock.

'Can't you see? He is a cattleman. Ask yourself, how welcome have these kind made us feel in their camps?' Looking eye to eye with Buck who now stood, he went on, 'I ask again, who are you and what do you want with us?'

'My name's James Buckley Armstrong, Buck to my friends so I guess you'd better call me Mr Armstrong.' Buck didn't soften his words with a smile. 'I was welcomed into this gentleman's camp for a cup of coffee. From you? I want nothing from you.'

'Jose, I won't have it.' The elder Navarro was angry and let a full load of that anger land on his son. 'I can't believe you are acting this way. It is clearly a strong tradition to make every visitor, whether friend or enemy, welcome in our camp. This is how it has always been and in my camp, it will always be.'

'Old man, you don't know these men. They carry pistols and have no reason not to use them. All too many of these cattle barons believe the land is for their livestock, not ours. You welcome the enemy into your camp; I will not. The lesson taught by the men herding cattle has not been forgotten. I will not sit with this man and drink coffee as if nothing has happened.' The anger in the young man's face didn't ease, and his posture remained rigid and unbending.

'What other men would these be?' Buck asked, hoping he'd get an answer and not more rage.

'Who knows? Just as every lamb looks like every other lamb to you, every cattleman looks like every other one. Big, self-important and ready to give orders, as if God made the land only for him.'

'Jose, you shame me.' Juan Navarro had given up. Turning to Buck he frowned. '*Señor*, you have my apologies. This one was turned away from a camp recently and now would do the same to everyone as if that will make everything better. He does not see that one's anger hurts only the person holding on to it. I am sorry.'

'Mr Navarro, there is no need to apologize. Not all cowmen like sheep and that's the truth. You've been the perfect host and I want to thank you for the coffee. I don't know what happened to make your son so determined to hate, but you're right: in the end, if he doesn't get rid of it, it'll eat him up.'

'Such self-righteous talk proves nothing. Being chased by big men on horses and having your flock shot into is reason enough for my anger.'

'When did this happen?'

'Oh, I'm sure it wasn't any of your employees. No, it'd be some strangers, wouldn't it? As if that mattered. Until I see otherwise, I'll believe all cattlemen are the same, ready to shoot and kill all who are not like them.'

'Unlike you who will welcome only travelers who are just like you. I am out here in this God-forsaken barren wasteland looking for cattle rustlers. Now, if you happened onto a passel of hardcases who didn't want to be seen and ran you off, then they just might be the ones I'm looking for. When did this happen and where was it?'

'See, just as I said,' the young sheepherder wasn't giving up. 'They were someone else and bad men, not a group of good, honest cattlemen; no. Go look for them all you want, you'll get nothing from me.'

Buck shook his head and after shaking the older man's hand again, tightened up the cinches and without another word, loped out of the camp and away from the bedded flock.

★ ★ ★

After making a dry camp a few miles south of the sheepherders' camp, Buck was up and riding again at daylight. Ranging back and forth, he covered a lot of country and it was getting close to noon before he found what he was searching for — sign that a small herd of cattle had been pushed along.

The first sign was cow pies that were

starting to dry out, two maybe three days, he thought. The breezes that sprung up nearly every evening as the sun went down and things cooled would, he reckoned, have wiped most all hoofprints out. Scouting around, he soon found other piles of dried cow dung. This gave him a direction if not a clear trail to follow. Slowly, ranging side to side, he followed what sign he found, often no more than a wisp of brown hair snagged on a twig or the odd hoofprint protected by a low-lying bush.

The sun was getting close to dropping behind the mountain range far out to the west when the ears of the big black stud flicked forward and his head came up. 'What is it?' he asked, not really expecting an answer. 'It's been a long dry march so far, so the chances are good that you got a smell of water. Let's see what we can see. Maybe, old friend, we won't have to drink that warm canteen water tonight.' Squeezing his knees a little, Buck let the horse have its head and sat back, ready for anything.

Before finding any indication of water, Buck caught a faint smell of smoke. Reining the big horse in, he stood in the stirrups and took a long look ahead. Nothing was seen in the failing light, but the breeze coming toward him once again had the smell of wood burning. He decided to take it easy and investigate the land ahead.

Pulling his mount to the side and up a small rise, he stopped before reaching the top and dropping the reins to the ground, made his way to the ridge. Keeping below the skyline and removing his hat, he carefully crawled forward. Below, in a small hollow, a bunch of cattle was clustered together by what looked to be a single rope corral. A small forest of willows on the far side was a sure sign of water. Probably a small spring. On this side, a short distance from the corral, a small fire was burning and two men were huddled around a hogtied critter. Buck had seen enough of these kinds of operations to recognize what it was — a couple of rustlers were working a brand using a running iron.

Settling back a bit, he watched as the calf, no more than a yearling, was released and herded back into the gather. As one of the men kicked the fire apart, the other rode around the corral, keeping his horse at a slow walk. Probably, Buck figured, making sure the corral was secure for the night. The horse was a bay with three white stockings, the off back leg being a darker color. From where Buck was, he couldn't make out anything distinctive about the rider, just another cowboy wearing typical cowboy gear: leather chaps to protect the rider's legs from brush and thorns; a weathered wide-brimmed, low-crowned hat, and a once-colorful kerchief around his neck. In the fading light he couldn't make out what color the neck scarf had once been, it could have been red or blue but now looked almost black.

As the light died away, Buck took in as much as he could, trying to decide what to do. These could be, he knew, simply hands from a nearby ranch, doing the job they were paid to do. He didn't know where the nearest ranch would be. Then again, these could be rustlers with a small bunch being held awhile for the brands to be reworked, or, if unbranded young stuff, for a new brand to be applied.

Trying to make up his mind, he saw the other man climb on to the back of a saddled horse and the two head out. Buck watched as they disappeared over a ridge far to the south-east. 'Now, don't that beat all,' he mumbled to himself.

Back in the saddle, he rode down into the swale in a circle, keeping the herd between him and the remains of the branding fire. Close up, he saw that about twenty or so head were penned up and that the cowboys had left the corral large enough so the cattle had room to spread out a bit. Most, from what he could see in the early starlight, were yearlings and maybe a few unweaned calves and their mothers.

Tying his horse with a slipknot to the rope corral, Buck walked around to the fire. Pulling the iron out of the coals he saw that it was a common running iron, a long straight rod with a curve at the heated end. Finding a stick of half burned wood, he blew on the hot coals until he got a flame and lit the end of the stick and used it like a torch.

He didn't have to go into the corral to see that one mother cow, standing protectively beside her calf, had a different brand than the little critter. He didn't recognize the new brand but the heifer was carrying the Rocking C mark. The rustlers were playing it smart. They'd brand the unbranded stock and then drive them to the railhead. Before getting close, the mother cows would be cut out and chased away. From the size of the calf, though, Buck thought it wouldn't be long before it was weaned and wouldn't need its mother anymore.

Stubbing out his burning branch, Buck took his horse around to the spring. After letting him drink, he climbed back into the saddle and thought about what to do next. The only thing to do, he decided, was to ride after the rustlers. It was only right, he thought, that he attempt to return the running iron.

5

The riders were long out of sight, but from what Matilda had told him Buck figured he was somewhere east of Coulter's Landing. It was likely that was where the two men were heading.

As late as it was, Buck wasn't surprised when he found few lights in the businesses along the main street. Most of the businesses along the street had probably closed before nightfall and the street, with the exception of two saloons, was dark and quiet. Lights from both of the taverns, one at the far end of the street and the other just down from the restaurant, spread out weakly over the wood plank sidewalk. The only other light showing was a faint lantern in the stable back the other way. Riding at a walk he passed first one and then the other saloon.

A weathered sign reading simply

SALOON hung from the porch over the double doors of the saloon furthest down the street. Buck draped the reins of his black to the far side of the three horses already tied to the rail. Taking a minute to look the horses over in the weak lantern light, he slipped the running iron into the saddle-bag hanging from the bay horse. None of the horses paid any attention and remained standing on three legs, obviously asleep.

Settling his heavy gunbelt to its usual position, he pushed through the doors and waited for his eyes to adjust to the sudden light. The polished wood bar ran along one wall and was backed by a large oil painting and shelves of bottled whiskeys. A beer barrel stood at one end, guarded by a portly bartender wearing a round-topped derby. Across the mahogany from the barkeep was a man who, from his clothing, a white shirt with the sleeves held up by black armbands and flat-heeled leather shoes, Buck took to be a shopkeeper. Possibly, he thought, a store clerk just sharing the day's gossip and having a sociable drink before ending his day.

Tables of various sizes took up the rest of the barroom floor, each with chairs haphazardly along its side. Other than the two men at the bar, the only occupants were a couple of cowboys sitting at one of the smaller tables, a whiskey bottle and glasses in front of them. After looking the newcomer over and not recognizing him, everyone but the bartender went back to their drinks.

'Evening,' the bartender came down to where Buck had stopped, leaning his left arm on dark wood bar. 'Get you a drink?'

'A nice cold glass of beer would be welcome,' he smiled. 'And some information would be even better.'

'Well, the beer is two-bits. I don't know about the information. Guess it depends on what you're looking to find out.' After pouring a tall heavy glass beer mug and swiftly knocking off its foamy head, he stopped across from

Buck and waited.

Buck looked around at the other customers and then, motioning to the barkeep, smiled again. 'Let's start off with your name, barkeep.'

'Well, you're about the only man in town that doesn't know Henry, the owner of this fine establishment,' the tubby man said laughing.

'Henry. Now I'll tell you. I'd appreciate it if you'd wipe off the top of the bar,' he said, his voice quiet and tinged with a hardness that wasn't matched by the smile. The bartender frowned.

'I don't know what you mean, stranger. The bar don't need wiped off.'

'Henry, in a minute I'm going to ask my questions and when I do I'd feel better if both your hands were visible. Now, holding a bar rag is one way to do that, wouldn't you say?'

Henry glanced quickly at the shopkeeper and then over to the other men. None of them was paying attention to anything but the drinks in front of them. Slowly, his eyes back on Buck's cold smile, he brought both hands and folded them on the bar top.

'Thank you, Henry. Now remember, any quick movement might not be advisable.' Taking a sip of beer, Buck let his voice grow a bit louder.

'Yeah. It's clear the herd is the work of some brand-changing skunks.' Now all eyes were on Buck. 'We came across them just about dark, a little after. Saw a coupla gents riding away and, as we hadn't had any supper, thought we'd use the fire they'd left behind.' The two men at the table exchanged glances and then turned their chairs to face the bar.

'Now I'm pretty much a stranger in these parts, but I did recognize the Rocking C brand on one cow in the bunch that was corralled by the spring.'

'So what?' one of the two men at the table asked with a sneer. 'The Rocking C is a big spread. Their stock is probably all over the place.'

'Yep, I reckon,' Buck agreed, taking

another sip of beer. 'The only problem is that the calf that was suckling this cow was wearing a different brand . . . a fresh brand.'

'Hey, there was some talk the other day about rustlers hitting the Randle ranch,' the shopkeeper down the bar said. 'Their foreman, Hank, was in town and mentioned it.'

'Well,' Buck nodded, 'I'd say this may just be the work of the bad guys. I left my crew there and came on into town to see what I could find. Guess I'll drop on out to Mrs Randle's place tomorrow and let her know what we found.' He had turned so he could see the two cowboys as well as the bartender. 'What I'm really wondering, Henry, is who belongs to that bay outside, the one with three white stockings? That looks a lot like the horse we saw leaving the little spring as we rode in.'

'Hey, now, wait just a minute. That bay out at the rail is mine, stranger. And I don't take to anyone calling me a rustler.' The man with the red kerchief tied loosely around his neck was now standing.

'Oh, I didn't call anyone anything,' Buck said, still standing relaxed but letting one hand drop to the butt of his Colt. With his thumb he flicked off the thong that held the gun in its holster. 'However, the gent that was seen riding that bay away from the fire was wearing leather chaps and a dark-colored neck scarf.'

Red kerchief let his body hunch a little, moving his right hand to rest on the butt of the gun that had been shoved behind his belt. From where Buck was standing, it looked like a Remington, probably either a .44 or maybe even a .40 caliber six-shooter.

'Stranger. I think you'd better make your words clear and if you're naming me a rustler, well, that'll be the biggest mistake of your short life.'

'Oh, gosh.' Buck's smile grew colder causing Henry to move slowly down the bar a ways. 'I wouldn't want to point any finger at an innocent man. I'm sure your momma didn't raise any cattle-thief, that is if you had a momma. But I'll tell you what. Let's take a look at your gear. Most cow-thieves I heard about all carry some kind of iron for reworking brands.'

Thinking about it, red kerchief slowly relaxed and smiled. Glancing down at his partner, he looked back at Buck. 'I'll tell you, stranger, what I'm gonna do. First we'll look at my saddle-bags and then I'm gonna shoot you. You're packing iron. It'll be a fair gunfight. My partner here will make sure of that, won't you, Lew?'

'Sure. Sure I will.' Pushing back his chair he stood beside red kerchief.

Nodding, Buck motioned toward the door. 'Then let us all retire to the hitch rail. Henry, would you mind bringing along that Greener you got somewhere behind the bar? I want to make sure old Lew here is as fair as he wants to be.'

No longer smiling, and careful not to let Buck get behind them, the two men moved to the doors and pushed through. Stepping off the boardwalk, red kerchief went around his horse and stopped.

'What do you have to say now, mister?' Buck demanded. He had followed the two men off the walk and stood to one side facing them. As red kerchief drew the running iron from his saddle-bag, his face turned white.

Turning to look at Buck, standing ready, he knew he'd been taken in.

'Damn you!' he cursed and, throwing the iron away, reached for his revolver.

6

Buck's draw was smooth and slightly behind the other's and his was the second shot heard by those still on the board-walk. Red kerchief's first shot, fired too quickly, raised dust in front of Buck's feet. Buck's shot hit true, centered on the third button of the man's shirt. Thrown back by the bullet, red kerchief knocked his partner's arm, making him drop his half drawn six-gun. Reaching to pick it up, he stopped and looked up to see the black end of Buck's Colt aimed at him.

'Go ahead.' Buck smiled thinly. 'There were two men riding away from that herd and one of them is dead. What do you have planned?'

'No. Don't shoot. I don't know anything about it. It was all his idea and I don't know anything about any rustling,' Lew's words were fast and almost running together.

'Here, what's going on? What's the shooting all about?' the call from down the street asked. Buck kept watching as Lew stood up and moved away from his pistol, as Sheriff Holt, pulling one suspender up over a blue and white striped nightshirt came running up. 'What's this all about? I'm the law here and we won't have any gunfights. Not in my town.'

'Why, good evening, Sheriff,' Buck said, his smile now calm and relaxed. Slowly he pushed the spent shell from his Colt and replaced it with one from his gunbelt.

'What's the meaning of this?' Frowning at Buck he turned to the men on the plank walk. 'Henry? What's this shooting all about?'

'Well, Sheriff, it seems this man was right. He claimed he'd seen that fellow there in the dirt ride away from a branding fire. Called him a rustler and when we found a running iron in his saddle-bags, well, he drew his gun. Too slow, I'd say.'

Holt walked around and bent over so he could see the fallen man's face. 'Anybody know him?' Nobody moved. Buck looked at Lew who was standing with both thumbs hooked in his belt. Lew didn't speak.

'You,' Sheriff Holt demanded, pointing at Buck. 'You come into town talking about a man you shot and now you've killed another man. What you do outside my town, I don't care, but I won't have gunplay on my streets.'

'Uh, Sheriff, this man didn't draw first. He was just protecting himself,' the storekeeper said.

'Clyde, you take care of the hotel and leave the sheriffing to me. Now you,' he said, pointing his finger once more at Buck's chest. 'I don't want your kind in town. Get your horse and ride.'

'Be careful, Sheriff, that your finger doesn't go off and get you in trouble.' Turning to the storekeeper he went on, 'You run the hotel?' When the man nodded, he added, 'Well then, let's go sign the book. I could use a night's sleep in a soft bed.'

Not giving the sheriff another glance the two men started walking off only to have Buck stop and turn to Lew. 'I'd suggest you do as the sheriff said. Get your horse and ride. And I think it'd be a good idea if you went on south, a long way south.'

Lew nodded and leaving his six-gun in the dust, untied and climbed into the saddle. Without a backward glance he spurred the horse into a trot.

'Goodnight, Henry, Sheriff,' Buck said, before following the hotel keeper down the street.

★   ★   ★

Coming awake early the next morning, Buck poured water from the pitcher and shaved. Pulling his last clean shirt from the saddle-bag he reminded himself to stop by the general store and replace the oldest of the two shirts he owned. The other one was getting a tad threadbare. Using his fingers to comb back his hair and settling his hat at the correct angle he left the room thinking about breakfast.

As early as it was, the fire in the town's only restaurant was blazing and the pot of coffee was hot and strong. The menu was chalked on a wide flat board that had been painted black. It simply listed three items; breakfast — $1, lunch — 50 cents, and supper — $1. Buck asked for coffee and breakfast.

Later, after a breakfast of eggs, thick slices of ham and fried potatoes topped off with large mugs of coffee, he relaxed in a rocking chair on the hotel porch and rolled a smoke. Buck felt ready for anything and gave some thought to what else he could do. Ride back to let Matilda know about the penned-up cattle he'd found was probably the first thing. Standing and stretching the kinks out of his back, he watched as a covered wagon came around the far end of the street and pulled up at the sheriff's office. Another sheepherder's wagon, he thought. Probably one of Navarro's friends.

Turning away, he started walking to the stable to saddle up but stopped when he heard his name called.

'Wait just a minute, Mr Armstrong.' Sheriff Holt's voice sneered loud and strong. 'You just stop right there.'

Turning, Buck watched the stout lawman leading a group of people coming down the middle of the dirt street. Walking slightly in front of the group and setting the pace, was a young man. Buck almost laughed as the short-legged sheriff nearly had to run to keep up. As the small crowd came closer he recognized the young stranger as the Basque sheepherder's son, Jose Navarro. Tipping his Stetson back he waited.

'Good morning, Sheriff,' he said, as the out of breath man stopped a short distance away. Buck's smile froze when Navarro, as angry as any man he'd ever seen, screamed at him.

'You bastard,' he shouted, his face dark and stiff with concealed fury. 'My father treated you like a guest and you killed him!'

7

His smile faded as Buck settled back on his heels and shook his head. 'Your father is dead?' he asked.

'It sounds like you,' Sheriff Holt chimed in, obviously having caught his breath. For the first time Buck noticed the short barreled shotgun the lawman held along one leg. 'It seems you're nothing but a killer. Ambushing a defenseless old man is just about your style, isn't it? You come into town with claims of leaving a dead man behind you, then last night push that cowboy into a gunfight, and now we hear how you'd already had your kill for the day.'

'Navarro, I don't know anything about your father being shot. Is he dead?'

'No, not quite,' he snarled, staring daggers at the big cowboy. 'Your bullet is in his chest. It took me all of the night before last and yesterday to get him in to the doctor. He hasn't regained consciousness yet. Your aim was a little off, but he is badly hurt. It doesn't look like you'll have to come back to shoot him again.'

'Now why would I shoot your pa? He treated me — '

'Yes,' the young man interrupted, 'he treated you as a guest in our camp and you paid him back by trying to kill him.'

'What have we here, Sheriff,' Hugh Hightower had ridden up unseen, stopping his horse slightly behind and to one side of where Buck stood.

'This killer is about to get run out of town, Mr Hightower.'

Buck, after glancing back at the horseman, returned his attention to Navarro. 'Why do you think I was the one who shot your father? I rode out of your camp day before yesterday.'

'You're another of those cattlemen who don't want sheep on the land, that's why.' He was no longer yelling, but his words came hard and fast. 'First you or your men take shots at me and shoot into my flock, trying to scare me off. Now you've gone one step too far, trying to kill my father. But it won't work. I have as much right to run my flocks on that land as anyone. You'll have to shoot me too, to get rid of my sheep.'

'What's this about shooting into your flocks?' the sheriff asked, his voice still loud enough to carry to the growing crowd of towns people. Election must be coming, Buck thought.

'I was chased away by a bunch of cowboys a few days ago. When I got out of their range, the bastards started shooting my sheep.'

'Because I was the next cowman you saw, you blamed me for that,' Buck said disparagingly. 'And now, because I was the last person in your camp you're going to blame me for shooting your pa. Man, I don't have any gang and if I did they certainly wouldn't be the kind that'd bother your sheep.'

'Hey, wait a minute.' Buck looked up to see the bartender, Henry. 'Didn't you say last night that you had left your crew out where you'd found that herd of rustled stock?'

The sheriff's shotgun came up, pointing it at Buck. 'That's all I need to hear, Mr Armstrong,' he said, the sneer back in his voice, 'we'll just take your Colt. The judge'll be riding in later this month and we'll let him decide what to do with you.'

'Nope, Sheriff,' Buck said, stepping back and grabbing the bridle of Hightower's horse and jerking its head around. Now behind the horse, he pulled his six-gun and aimed up at the rider. 'Don't think about taking part in this, cowboy,' he warned. Calling out to the sheriff he shook his head. 'OK, Sheriff, you've shown how brave and officious you can be and the town's voters are impressed. But I'm not. Now point that short gun somewhere else.'

Cursing, the portly badge-toter lowered the shotgun.

'Sheriff, if I remember right,' Buck continued, still holding the bridle, 'you don't have any jurisdiction outside of town. And as for this man's pa, I don't know anything about it, so it's my word against his. Now, I'm going to go see just how bad the old man is, and I don't recommend that you or any of your friends try to stop me.'

Holstering his revolver, Buck released his hold on the bridle. 'Now you listen to me, stranger,' the lawman said, still holding his shotgun at his side. 'You're right. I can't do much about what you did outside of town. But my recommendation to you is that you get your horse and ride out of our town. We don't want your kind here. Ride out and don't come back.'

Buck saw that the round-faced sheriff had the backing of those people standing in the street behind him and nodded. 'All right. I can't fight the entire town. Navarro, I'm sorry about your pa and hope the doctor can help him. But I want you to know, I didn't have anything to do with shooting him or your sheep.'

Backing up, before turning to the stable, he nodded to the sheriff, 'Good morning, Sheriff.'

8

Buck hated to tell Matilda about his shooting the rustler and didn't mention his planting the running iron in the man's saddle-bag. But he had to explain how he came about finding the cattle and knew that if he didn't talk about the gun battle, someone would. Hearing this news didn't make the young ranch owner feel better and only seemed to add to her troubles. He understood when she explained that she'd had a visit from the banker, Harvey Blount.

'He had the loan paper and I recognized Virgil's signature. Buck, I don't have the money and won't until I can get a herd to the railhead. Hank says that won't be for another month at least. The bank loan is due in just a few days. I don't know what I'm going to do.'

Buck frowned. 'We can get around that loan if you can get into town and send a telegraph. The professor will send you the money. I'll have him take it out of my account. I can't go back into town so you'll have to do it.' To explain why, he told her about Navarro's charge that he'd shot the elder sheepherder and the sheriff's banning him from town.

They were sitting around the big kitchen table and didn't hear anyone ride in. The first Matilda knew she had company was when someone pounded on the front door. Hurrying to answer, she quickly returned followed by Hugh Hightower.

'I hurried out, Matilda,' he said, glaring at Buck, 'hoping I'd get here before he did. Stranger, get on your feet and ride out,' he ordered, stepping closer and letting his hand fall on a gun butt.

'Hugh! Stop that. This man is a guest in my home and I'll be the one who decides who stays and who goes. Now, either behave like a gentleman or leave.'

'Matty, this man's a killer. He's killed at least three men since coming into the valley. I wouldn't be surprised if he didn't have a hand in the rustling that's been bothering you.'

'Why would that matter to you, Hugh?'

'This gunny is bad news and I want to protect you.' He softened his tone. 'Matty, I keep telling you that you need a strong man to help you during these hard times. Keeping trash grubline riders like this one away is what I'm talking about.'

'Mr Hightower,' Buck smiled and, pushing back his chair, stood. 'I don't know who you think you are, but calling a man names won't get you anything but a bullet or a broken jaw.'

'Stop it, both of you! I won't have it. Now, Hugh Hightower, this man is my guest and was sent by a friend to help me. I trust him. On top of that, my name is Matilda Randle, not Matty.'

'Friend of a friend or not, this man's a killer. If you won't listen then I can't help you. But remember, I've always been your neighbor and am willing to give you all the help you need. I can help you with men or money. Yes,' he said at her look, 'Blount mentioned the bank loan that Virgil had made and I also heard about the IOUs that Hubbard is holding. If you don't have the money, I can clear that up for you. All I want is to help you. This ranny won't be here long and I will. Think about it.' Jamming his hat back on his head, he stomped out of the kitchen and, slamming the front door behind him, stepped into the saddle. Jerking the reins around he galloped out of the yard.

★ ★ ★

Buck wrote out a brief message to the professor and while Matilda rode into town to put it on the telegraph, he thought he'd ride out to tell Hank about the penned cattle. Saddling up his black horse and throwing the rig on Matilda's dun, he was relaxing on the porch waiting for her when he spotted a small party of riders coming up the road. As they neared the ranch yard, Buck could make out that these were not cattlemen. Nearly all were wearing bibbed coveralls and straw hats, their heavy work boots were not suitable for stirrups. For that matter, all of the horses were of a big heavy strong breed better cut out for pulling a plow or wagon than wearing a saddle.

Coming to a halt, they lined up facing the porch and sat silently staring at Buck. The big cowboy took his time, looking them over each in turn neither smiling nor giving any other indication of welcome. Buck didn't have the typical viewpoint of most livestock ranchers; he treated them just as he would any rider, as neither friend nor foe until they proved themselves. This bunch, however, didn't hide their feelings . . . they didn't like Buck.

'Why Mr Cooder, gentlemen,' Matilda said, coming out of the house, pulling on a pair of thin leather riding gloves, 'I didn't hear you all ride in. Please, step down and have a cup of coffee.'

The men nodded to the woman and most even removed their hats. 'Miz Randle, we thank you for the invite, but we're not here on a social visit. There is a matter we wish to discuss with you.' The speaker was the oldest of the group, his shoulders once broad and square had taken on the droop common to a man who had worked hard for too many years. His clothes, like most worn by the others, were clean although the knees of his pants were a shade or two lighter than the rest of the cloth. Blue eyes shaded by overgrown eyebrows were the brightest part of his weather-browned face. The man's forehead was white and almost pasty looking from where his hat sat. Below that his sun-browned lined face was marked by creases and age-wrinkles, some, Buck thought, deep enough to hide a buggy in. His hair was thinner on top and where it had once been mousy brown now had lots of white showing up.

'Mr Cooder, please step down and tell me what brought you all out here today?' Matilda smiled, her words showing real friendship.

'Miz Randle, the problem is men like the one sitting there on your porch,' the farmer said, making no attempt to soften his words and pointing at Buck. 'For as long as we've been in the south valley, you ranchers have treated us fairly. Lately, however, things have changed. We can't take much more of it.'

'I'm not sure what you're talking about, Mr Cooder. However I will say that Buck is here to help me, not cause my friends trouble. You are my friends, aren't you?'

'We thought so. Your father, unlike some, welcomed us to the valley and was always a good market for our wheat and oats. More than once he paid for a crop before it was even planted, just so we could afford to buy the seed. But that's changed since he passed on. Now we have cattle being driven through our crops, our irrigation chutes at the river destroyed and salt blocks thrown in our ponds. The worst, though, was having our women afeared to come to town, afraid of being harassed by saddle tramps and other riffraff. We have complained to Sheriff Holt but all he can do is tell us there was nothing he could do. We are bringing the problem to you.'

'What can I do? Why are you laying this at my door?'

'Because it is your cattle we find in our fields in the morning. The cowboys who yell and make rude comments to our women may not be yours, but they certainly ain't farmers.'

'Mr Cooder,' and anger clipped her words, 'I guarantee you that none of my hands have run any of my beef onto your fields. And not one of my men is the kind to hassle any woman.'

'Yes, I expected you to say that but it is just possible that this is happening without your knowing it. But it is happening. The cattle are from your ranch.'

'I swear to you that none of this is coming from the Rocking C.'

One of the other farmers, a younger version of Cooder, scoffed at her words. 'We'd find it easier to believe if that killer wasn't sitting so calmly and quietly on your front porch, ma'am,' he said with disdain.

'Young man,' Buck said, standing, and looking eyeball to eyeball with the mounted man. 'You're coming awfully close to calling Mrs Randle a liar. And naming me a killer is dangerous talk, isn't it? I mean if it is true.'

The young man's face paled and he carefully put both hands in view. 'I'm only saying what we was told by the sheriff.' His voice had lost all traces of bravado.

'Miz Randle,' Cooder went on as if the boy had not spoken, 'we've said our piece. From now on we'll be trying to protect our crops. Any of your cattle that come onto our land will be shot. When we need to go to the market, we'll take our women into Brisby. Until we get some honest law in the valley, we'll have to protect ourselves. That goes for your gunmen, too,' he said, glaring in Buck's direction. 'C'mon men, we've said what we came to say.'

9

Nothing was said between the widow and Buck as they rode out to the holding ground to find Hank. After telling the ranch foremen where to find the penned-up beeves he stood back and listened while Hank gave his boss an update on the round-up. Getting a herd to the railhead and waiting buyers, he said, would take another week. Far too long to make it possible for Matilda to meet the payment on the loan and satisfy Blount.

Riding to town, Buck wondered if the ranch's credit was sufficient to get an extension. 'I doubt it,' Matilda shook her head. 'We've always made it a point to pay for things as we go along. Even when we needed to borrow, we'd go to the bank over in Brisby. The banker there is an old friend of Pa's and he'd always done his business with him. That didn't sit well with Mr Blount. I doubt he'd think it was in his best interest to extend the loan payment.'

'Well, there's enough in my account to cover this month's payment and your herd should be delivered by the next due date.'

'Yes. I'll be able to pay that note off, once the herd is sold. I still can't believe Virgil would take out a loan without telling me. I really appreciate your advancing the money. Thank you.'

'What do you plan to do about the gambler's IOU? I doubt if that kind of debt is legal, if you just wanted to tell the gambler to forget it.'

Matilda rode for a while without speaking. 'I suppose I could turn my back on it, but what would that do to the ranch's reputation? No, I guess I'll have to make good on it. By the way, what are you going to do about the sheriff telling you not to come back into town?'

'Oh, I guess I'll just ignore it. That wire has to be sent and I think I'll ask about having the state send a marshal over, a real lawman,' he said with a bark of laughter. 'Anyway, this big-footed horse of mine has a shoe that needs replacing.'

★   ★   ★

The telegraph office was in the hotel and while Buck sent his two messages Matilda sat at a table in the restaurant having a late lunch. Joining her, Buck ordered a cup of coffee and sat back to enjoy her company.

'That should get delivered this afternoon or maybe tomorrow morning. Your note is due when — Friday? That'll give us three or four more days. I'll have to come back in early Friday morning and pick up the draft. Somehow I don't think Banker Blount will like it much, but he'll have to accept it.'

'You'll be repaid once the herd is sold,' she smiled, and then looking over Buck's shoulder let the smile fade.

'Here comes Sheriff Holt, Buck.'

'Well, you don't care who you are seen with do you, Miz Randle?' Holt said self-importantly as he came close to the seated couple. 'Didn't I tell you that you're not welcome, cowboy? The good people here don't want killers and back-shooters dirtying up their town.'

Buck finished taking a sip of coffee and then, placing the cup carefully in its saucer, looked up at the round-faced lawman. 'Sheriff Holt,' he said, his voice hard and loud enough for others to hear every word, 'this is the only warning you're likely to get. Call the wrong man a killer or a back-shooter and you're liable to have to eat the words. Now, if you can prove your statement, let's have it. If not, be careful.'

The man's face blanched at Buck's words, his small, beady eyes standing out in his soft-looking face. Before he could respond, Buck stood up, towering over the man, his eyes cold. 'Can you back up your words, or not? If you can't, you'd better be making tracks out of my sight before I get real mad.'

Buck's fierce look convinced the sheriff who quickly turned and all but ran for the door. Matilda laughed at the sight of the pompous man's departure. The other customers in the place, smiling or not at the sheriff's retreat, hastily turned back to their own business.

'You have made an enemy, you know. Holt has been the town's sheriff for a long time. I think it's because nobody else will take the job. He may be ridiculous, but he is a proud man. Watch out for him, Buck.'

'I guess I'm a little irritated that someone like him has any authority. His not bothering to look into your husband's death should have the voters checking their hole card. One of the telegrams I sent was to the governor's office asking for a marshal to be sent in. That may make our sheriff even angrier.'

Paying for the lunch and his coffee,

Buck left Matilda who wanted to make some purchases at the general store. Untying the big black horse, he swung into the saddle and headed down the street to the stable and the blacksmith's forge behind it. The smithy was hard at it, hammering with strong blows the red-hot end of a horseshoe against the massive anvil. Sweat poured off the man as he swung the hammer with a clang, flattening out the shoe. Not quite as tall as Buck, the black-haired smith was bigger in almost every way. His chest, only covered by a black leather vest, was broad and muscular. Arms the size of some men's thighs flexed as he raised the five-pound hammer only to bring it back down with great force. Holding the shoe with a pair of tongs, he returned the metal to the fire as its color cooled from a cherry-red to a rosy gray.

'Morning.' Buck had paused until the hammering stopped and the smith waited for the shoe to heat up. 'Do you have time this afternoon to check the shoes on my horse? I think the right front is wearing a little thin.'

The blacksmith looked up as Buck swung down. 'Yeah, I can get to it soon as I replace the rim on that wagon tire there. Leave the nag tied to the fence and I'll get to it.'

'Well, I'd do that, but this old horse has a bad habit of biting anyone who gets too close. It'd probably be better if I hung around to make him mind his manners.'

'Naw. Any horse tries to take a bite of me learns quickly how bad an idea that is. This hammer between his eyes'll teach him who not to mess with.'

'And then I'd have to teach you not to mess with my horse. That is if he let you get close enough to do him any harm.'

'You'd teach me? Little man, the sun hasn't come up on the day that'll happen. Say, wait a minute. Ain't you the fellow that shot that sheepherder? You hardcase cow nurses think you can do just anything you want, don't you?

105

Maybe it's time for someone to teach you what's what.'

'Nope, all I want is to have the shoes on my horse taken care of.' Buck watched as the man took the shoe out of the forge and dropped it sizzling into a bucket of water.

'Mister, you are about to learn what happens when someone I like gets hurt. I'm gonna hurt you,' he whispered menacingly, as he walked toward the big cowboy. Buck stepped back and drew his Colt.

'I don't think so. A bullet in the leg will put a helluva stop to your fixing the shoes on my horse.'

'Are you going to shoot me too, killer?' someone behind Buck asked. Looking over his shoulder he saw the young man who'd been with the farmer, Cooder, standing with a three-tined pitchfork in his hands. 'Why don't you just put that pistol away and stand up to Calvin? Let's see how you do without a gun in your hand.' He said, laughing and jabbing threateningly at the cowboy's back.

Buck looked back at the blacksmith who stood with his arms crossed, smiling. Shaking his head, Buck walked his horse over and looped the reins over a fence rail. Removing his Stetson, he let it dangle by the chinstrap from the black's saddle horn. Unbuckling his gunbelt he hung it with the hat.

'You better hang on to that pitchfork, youngster. You might need it.'

'Come and get it, back shooter,' the smith snarled, his body in a crouch, his calloused hands curled into rough-looking fists, as he slowly moved closer to Buck.

10

Calvin almost ended the battle with the first blow. Buck took the first one on his shoulder, being able to only just duck out of the way of the fist. Back pedaling, he tried to get his balance, but the man was on him and didn't let the cowboy get set. Evading the blacksmith's iron-hard fists as much as he could, Buck misjudged the attack and the second jolt was to his rib cage. Knocked flat on his back, he quickly rolled away from the big man. Laughing at him in the dust, Calvin stood, waiting for him to get up. Buck saw the smithy wasn't even breathing hard.

As strong as Buck was, this man was a lot stronger. It had been a long time since he'd been in a stand-up fistfight and this wasn't going his way. Taking as much time as he could, he slowly came to his feet.

'You aren't so much without your gun, are you, killer?' someone behind Buck laughed.

Wincing at the pain in his chest, Buck raised his fists and began circling the big blacksmith. Jabbing with a quick left, he saw that for all his size, Calvin was slow, a big, slow tree of a man. Another jab clipped his whiskery chin, brought the smith's roundhouse left fist around. Buck ducked and came up inside, landing a solid blow square on the man's chin. Shaking his head, the blacksmith grinned.

'Is that the best you can do, little man?'

Buck didn't waste time answering but started to circle again. If he could get a couple more like that, maybe he had a chance. Slow to react, the big man might be, but he was quicker when he needed to be. Buck flinched to the right when he saw the man's left coming at him, only to run into a clenched right fist. Once again he found himself on his back in the street's dust.

'Stop it!' he heard a woman's cry. 'Calvin, you stop fighting right now! You'll kill him.' Now on his knees, Buck shook his head, trying to stop the ringing.

'Aw, Sis, this is the hardcase that ambushed Jose's pa. Let Calvin have some fun with him,' young Cooder protested.

'I ain't through with him yet,' Calvin growled, standing with his legs firmly planted, waiting for Buck to get up.

Taking a quick glance around, Buck saw that quite a crowd had gathered to watch. Slowly he came to his feet and with his fists up circled his opponent, looking for an opening. Staying out of the smithy's range, Buck knew if he took another wallop like the last one he wouldn't get up. Jabbing as he circled, he kept his feet moving, ready for any strike. A couple of his jabs landed on the side of Calvin's chin, one slamming against the side of the big man's ear when he ducked. None of the punches seemed to bother the blacksmith.

Calvin's grin grew as he turned, watching as the cowboy circled around. 'Dammit, stand still,' he snarled, hurling his fist once more at Buck's head. Seeing it coming, Buck danced back and then reversed and, moving inside, slammed first his left fist and then his right, landing both on the unshaven chin knocking the blacksmith on his back.

Buck moved back and used the time to catch his breath, watching as the smithy rolled over and got his feet under him. Standing and shaking his head, neither man was ready to continue when Buck was pushed from behind. Off balance, he fell toward Calvin who reacted with a backhand that smacked Buck's head around.

On his hands and knees, Buck let his head hang down and barely heard the yells and roars of the crowd aimed at whoever had pushed him. Slower than ever, he stood up. Putting up his fists once more and ignoring the sounds of the crowd, he started his circling.

Almost stumbling as he moved, Buck knew he'd have only one more chance before it'd be all over.

Calvin simply batted the jabs at his face away. Standing solidly he could see that Buck was on his last legs. He could wait. Turning slowly as Buck circled he smiled and let one work-hardened fist fall a bit, enticing the other man to swing. Buck's left fist snaked out and as the smithy's dropped hand came up, Buck saw the opening and launched his right. Bringing it up from the ground and throwing all his weight behind it, his knuckles contacted fully on Calvin's chin. Falling back from the blow the smithy's head struck the iron anvil. Sprawled out, he didn't move.

11

Buck stood for a moment, catching his breath before turning to the now quiet crowd. Looking directly at young Cooder, he smiled. 'Now who was it that pushed me?' he asked, as evilly as he could.

Cooder, his face white with fear, turned and, pushing through the mob, disappeared.

'Mister?' Buck turned to find a young woman, no more than a girl, looking up at him. 'He didn't mean to push you,' she said, letting her eyes drop in embarrassment.

Buck glanced beyond the girl at others who had watched the fight. Slowly, with the excitement over, the citizens began to go about their business leaving only a few anxious to see what would happen next. Standing beside Matilda Randle was Hugh

Hightower. Matilda's face was flushed and strained.

'He didn't?' Buck asked quizzically, looking closely at the girl and seeing the family resemblance. 'Is this the same fellow who stood behind me with a pitchfork forcing the fight?'

Stammering with more embarrassment, the girl simply nodded. 'He's just hot-headed. And the Navarros have been friends of our family since we got here. He really isn't cruel or mean, just angry.'

'Buck, I'd like to talk with you when you're finished there,' said Matilda, still full of nervous tension. 'I'll be at the horses.' Turning she walked away with Hightower at her side leaving Frank and two other young men. Smirking, Frank nodded to Buck and nudging the man next to him, followed his father.

'Young lady . . . what's your name, anyhow?'

'Elizabeth Cooder.'

'Yeah, I figured. I've met your father and his friends and now I've met you

114

and your brother. A very angry family, aren't you, and blaming your troubles on Matilda's crew. And myself, of course. Well, Miss Cooder, I'll tell you just as I've tried to persuade everybody . . . I did not shoot the sheepherder or his boy's sheep.'

'The sheriff thinks you did and until he learns differently, so does my pa. And,' she said, with pride behind her words, 'so do I.'

'Elizabeth, come away now.' The youngster who had been standing with the Hightowers put his hand on the girl's arm. 'It does no good, standing here in the street talking to this man.'

Nodding in agreement and giving Buck a last look of displeasure, Elizabeth Cooder let the young man walk her away.

Buck watched the couple walk off and, after checking to see that Calvin was breathing, dipped his head in a nearby water trough. Combing his hair with his fingers and brushing at his clothes, he buckled on his gunbelt and settled his hat in place before stepping into the saddle and going to look for Matilda. What he really wanted, he thought was a hot bath and a drink of good whiskey, but that could wait a bit.

★　★　★

Hightower and Matilda were sitting on chairs on the hotel porch as Buck rode up. Tying the reins loosely to the rail, he went up the three broad steps and stood facing them. After nodding in Hightower's direction, he put his fingers to his hat, as a greeting to Matilda.

'You said you wanted to talk,' he smiled, lounging back against the porch railing. The pain in his chest was fading so he didn't believe a rib had been broken. When the smithy had hit him, he was sure the whole side of his chest had been caved in, but now the main pain was the throbbing in his head.

'Yes, I do.' She turned to Hightower

and said, 'Thank you, Hugh. But I think I'd better handle this.'

The horse rancher signaled his agreement and with a last mocking smile at the standing cowboy, walked off down the boardwalk.

'Buck, I don't know what to think. You have offered to help me with the bank and I appreciate that, but, well, since you came into the valley there have been at least two men shot, one of them a defenseless old sheepherder. The other, I'll admit, might have been a rustler, but we'll never know, will we?' It was a statement, not a question. 'And now picking a fight with the blacksmith. I honestly don't know what to believe.'

'I see your beau, Hightower, didn't waste any time,' he said gently.

'He's not my beau.' Anger brought more color to her face. 'Hugh is just looking out for me. After all, I've known him since I was little and I don't know you at all. Of course he's concerned for me and did talk to me on the things he's worried about.'

'For the record, Mrs Randle,' he let a little bite creep into his words, 'the rustler was stealing your cows and he did make his draw first. As far as that old sheepherder is concerned, I didn't shoot him. Wasn't anywhere near his camp when it happened. The fight? Well, I didn't start that and was damn lucky to walk away when it was finished.'

'Maybe all you say is right and Hugh is wrong. I'm just not sure.'

'Well, missy, you just do whatever you think is best for you. I was asked by my good friend the professor to help you if I could and that's what I'm doing.'

'Buck, I'm very grateful for your offer to pay the bank payment, but you won't have to. Hugh says he'll take care of it and I can repay him when I sell my herd.'

Buck studied the toe of his boots for a minute and then smiled down at the woman. 'All right. It's your call.

Now, if you'll excuse me I think it's time for a drink and a bath.' Touching his hat brim toward the lady, he picked up the reins and swung back into the saddle.

12

While Buck enjoyed the luxuriously steaming-hot bath water, he had the dirt from the street beaten and shaken out of his clothes. Once again he didn't know what to do. He had offered Matilda money to help her out of one problem and had been turned down. The rustling, at least as far as one curly wolf was concerned, was taken care of. He could, he supposed, have a talk with the man holding the gambling IOUs, but that might be a problem better left to Matilda to work out. What else could he do? Leaving the valley without feeling he'd done as the professor had asked was not an easy decision, but . . . what else was there?

His black horse was ready for traveling. Riding away from the hotel and Matilda, he had gone back to the stable and the blacksmith's shop.

Someone had poured a pail of water over the smith and Buck found him sitting with his back to the tree stump that held the anvil, holding his head.

'I have to say,' Buck smiled through his words, 'getting hit by you is not something I'd recommend to my worst enemy.'

Calvin moved his head slowly as if he was afraid it'd break. 'What the hell do you want?'

'Why, my horse still needs shoeing. That little fight didn't put you out of business, did it?'

'You'd come back here, after doing what you did? And expect me to put shoes on your horse?'

'Hey, my horse didn't do anything to you. To tell the truth, if it hadn't been for that anvil, I'd be the one holding my head. You're one tough man.'

Staring up at the rider, the smith thought for a minute and then smiled. 'You are not so easy yourself. Here, help me up.' He held out a big paw of a hand. Buck swung down and pulled the man up. 'Is your horse as mean as you said?'

'He's got a mean streak, for sure. Somehow he puts up with me, but he can get rambunctious around anyone else.'

'Damn. All right, you hold him and I'll fix his shoes.'

Buck held the big black's bridle and Calvin lifted first one leg and then the other, inspecting the shoes. The man was big and tough, but his hands were surprisingly gentle as he ran them down each leg.

'Have to replace that one,' he allowed, 'a couple nails in another and you'll be right.' Standing and looking at Buck, he thought for a minute and then asked, 'Is it true? Did you shoot old Juan Navarro like they say you did?'

'Nope. The old man shared a cup of coffee with me and when his boy came into camp . . . well, I decided not to take him up on his invitation to spend the night. I rode on and made a dry camp a few miles away. Didn't hear any shots and didn't know there had been any until a day or so later when young Navarro came in accusing me. I liked him, the old man, I mean.'

'OK, then. I'll fit a new shoe on your horse.'

Buck stood by the black's head, stroking his broad forehead while Calvin sized a shoe and nailed it in place. Accepting a few coins in payment, the blacksmith nodded his thanks and without another word went back to the bellows, forcing air into the forge, building up his fire.

With one foot in the stirrup, Buck stopped and watched a man come riding down the street toward him.

'Hey, there. Where can I find Miz Randle?' the Rocking C foreman asked pulling to a stop. 'We got to that pen you told us about a tad late. The cattle had been moved out.'

'Damn,' Buck swore, grimacing. 'I'll bet it was that fool partner of the guy I shot, Lew. He probably met up with the rest of the gang. That's how they got the jump on you. Those cows'll be sold by now. I should've gone back then, instead of grabbing a night in a real bed.'

'Well, we know where they went and they couldn't have been traveling very fast. I followed the trail left by the rustlers. They're heading for the railhead at Big Valley. That's where we'll be taking our herd. There're always a few buyers hanging out there this time of year. More later in the fall when ranchers from all over this part of the state make their drives.'

'Hank, how far south is that railhead?' asked Buck as he swung into the saddle.

'From here? It's maybe two days' ride, I expect. With a fast horse, a rider might make it in a bit less.'

Thinking about it, Buck shook his head. 'They don't know me there, so if I were to come riding in nobody would pay me any attention.'

'Well, unless Miz Randle says different, I can't go. After all, it's only a dozen or so yearlings and young stuff. They'd already started dropping off the mother cows so those that reach the buyers will have the right brands on their hip. I just wanted to let Miz Randle know what I'd found and this is almost on my way back to the holding ground. I still got a round-up to take care of.'

Buck told Hank he'd most likely find his boss at the hotel. At least that was the last place he'd seen her. As the foreman reined away, Buck called out a question. 'How far south would I find the sign of the rustled stock?'

'About two hours or so, a little south-east of here. The river thins out just before it joins the Red River,' Hank pointed. 'That one is more dirt than water, too thick to drink but too wet to walk on, they say. This time of year a herd can be forded almost anywhere along there. You watch, you won't miss the mess those young beeves made making the crossing. The railhead is just a few miles beyond.' Tipping his hat, the foreman reined around and gigged his horse on up the street.

★   ★   ★

It was well over two hours before Buck found any sign of a small herd being pushed along. The sun was close to dropping below the horizon when he found the hoofprints. Even then, with dusk starting to make it difficult, he might not have found the trail except for the bawling of a cow. Turning to find the troubled animal, he came up on a mean-looking cow walking with her head down, looking about ready to drop.

'Hey, bossy,' Buck murmured. 'What are you doing out here, trying to be dinner for a bunch of coyotes?' Coyotes wouldn't bother a full-grown beef and rarely even try to bring down anything but a newborn calf. But from the looks of the cow, death wasn't far away. Thin, even in the failing light, Buck could see her ribs sticking out of her heaving sides. Hearing the horse coming up behind her, she stopped and turned her head, swinging her wide-spaced horns toward any danger. Buck pulled his horse to a halt.

'Well, horse, what do you say we make a dry camp right about here? There's enough water in the canteen to make things a little better.' Once again the horse didn't pay any attention.

Camp was quickly set up. First he dropped a rope around the cow's horns and snubbing her head to a nearby bush, poured a good measure of water into his cooking pan. Picketing his horse, he shared more of the water with the black stud. After a quick supper cooked over a small fire, he filled his coffee pot with enough for tonight and in the morning and gave the rest to the tethered cow. He wasn't sure, but this heifer looked a lot like the one he'd seen in the rope corral. There was no reason he could think of for her to be following the rustled herd. If so, maybe he could make her trip a little easier.

13

The next morning Buck hazed the heifer along as fast as he dared. Late in the morning they came up on the river and he could see what Hank had meant about it becoming thin. Flowing out over the flats, the water spread out wide and shallow. Both the big black and the heifer quickly drank their fill.

A short ride along the winding river, with the tracks left by the young stuff, led Buck and the momma cow to where the herd had forded the bigger river. Far from the color red, the water was a muddy brown. Crossing, the water level didn't reach anywhere near the bottoms of his stirrups. The rustled herd wouldn't have had any problems getting over at least this time of year. Trunks of dead trees stuck in the bottom mud proved that at times the force of this river was a lot different than what it was now, in late summer.

On the other side, the heifer didn't hesitate but kept moving. Buck, following behind, now believed they were making better time and wasn't surprised when, early in the afternoon and standing high in the stirrups, he could make out the holding pens at the Big Valley junction. The heifer was all but running as she smelled her calf.

Reaching one of the smaller pens, the cow stood with her head between the rails and bawled. Buck climbed tiredly out of the saddle and watched as a calf pushed through the small herd to nuzzle the heifer. Nodding with satisfaction, he removed the saddle from the black horse, let him roll and then led him to the water barrel.

'Hey, boy. What the hell are you doing?' Buck looked up as a big man wearing a store-bought suit came striding up. Scowling, the man pointed to the hip-boned heifer standing outside the pen and demanded an explanation. 'Those pens are for cattle being sold here, boy. Now you just get that sorry looking beast out o' there.'

'Nope,' Buck said, dipping his kerchief into the water barrel and then wiping his face and hands. After plunging his head into the barrel and letting the water drip, he looked up at the bullying man. 'I don't guess I will, at least not yet,' he went on, looking the self-important man up and down.

Before the blustering man could react, another well-dressed man, likewise wearing a suit and high-topped shoes came up and asked quietly what all the yelling was about. Before the blustering man could respond, Buck cut in.

'Just looking for the gents that brought that jag of young stuff in,' he said, putting out his hand. 'I'm James Buckley Armstrong, Buck to my friends. That heifer there is wearing the Rocking C brand and her calf has one that's slightly different. That doesn't seem right to me.'

'Well, I'd say there is something odd about it, wouldn't you, Thompson?' the man asked shaking Buck's hand and looking at the first man. 'My name is Collins and both Thompson and I are cattle buyers. Fact is, I'm waiting word on when the Randle herd is due.'

Strolling over to stand near the heifer, he shook his head. 'Thompson, I must say, there is something strange about this little bunch and I think I mentioned that when they came in. Now, looking at the two brands, I say, not too smart of you to doubt it, don't you think?'

Glancing toward the small building that served as both rail-master's office and waiting-room, Buck saw three or four other men start walking over, curious to see what all the yelling was about. He smiled as he recognized one of the men.

Turning back to the cattle buyer, he said quietly, 'Mr Collins, I'm afraid I've got a little problem to settle and if you know the Rocking C, maybe you're just

131

the man I need to back me.'

'Oh, I know the Randle family all right. Virgil and Matilda. And in his time, the old man, too. I've been buying their herds for quite a while, ever since Old Jim Coulter first came out here. That was before there was a railhead anywhere near here. He used to have to drive . . . well, that isn't the issue now, is it?' he finished, looking up to see the men now standing facing Buck.

Buck, having released the reins of his horse, smiled at the one he recognized. 'Well, look who's here. It's Lew, isn't it? Fancy meeting you again. Seems you didn't get my message.' Carelessly placing his hand of the butt of his belt gun, Buck went on, 'Now I'm going to ask these fine gentlemen to witness this. Mrs Randle's Rocking C has been missing a few head, and I have proof that the yearlings and weaners in that pen are from her herd. Seems likely that certain hardcases have been changing the brand and some buyer here has been taking them. Now, I'm not about to point the finger at anyone, but I think I could spit on at least one of the rustlers right now. He knows who he is because he was there when I caught his partner with a running iron in his hand. And I can probably guess who has been buying the stolen stock.'

Collins, seeing the direction of Buck's stare, moved to one side out of the line of fire. 'Now, boy, I don't think any gunplay is necessary.'

'What do you mean?' the first complaining cattle buyer said, not noticing the tension that was filling the men's bodies. 'You're declaring that some buyer has been taking stolen stock? I'll have you know none of us here is guilty of that.'

'No?' Buck asked, never taking his eyes off the men facing him across the water barrel. One, holding his rifle in one hand with the barrel pointed at the ground, looked at the young rancher with a vacant stare. The other slowly removed a glove from his right hand and let that hand drop casually on the cedar handles of his belt gun. 'I'll bet that if either of those rannies there would talk, they'd point right at the buyer I'm talking about. But that's OK. I guess I'll just have to hurt one of them before I ask about that. You there, Lew, what can you tell me about this deal?'

'Hurt one of us, boy?' Lew said, laughing, as his fingers slowly tightened about his pistol grips. 'You can't just ride in here making brags like that, claiming me or my friends are rustlers? You can't do that and then expect to ride out.'

'Yep, I just did do that. And it's a claim I can prove. All we got to do is go look at the brand on that heifer I just brought in and the brand on her calf. You dropped her too soon. Any fool can see her calf isn't fully weaned yet.'

Hearing that, Lew stopped laughing and, without saying another word, in one smooth movement, his long-barreled pistol came clear of the holster. At the same time, the man with the rifle brought it up, his finger finding the trigger. Buck could only react, pulling his six-gun and firing without aiming and at the same time, throwing his body to the left.

14

The silence following the sudden gunfire was thick. For a time nobody moved and no one said anything. Slowly, realizing he had been holding his breath, Buck exhaled. Still with his handgun pointing in the direction of the rustlers, he watched as the rifleman, his eyes still staring, unhurriedly doubled over, falling first to his knees and then falling flat on his face. Looking down he saw his shot had gone true, taking Lew squarely in the chest. The third man stood with both hands shoulder high and empty, his face a pasty gray.

'Don't shoot me. I didn't sign on for this; don't shoot. I ain't going for my gun,' he babbled.

'I'll tell you what' — Buck used his Colt as a pointer, jabbing it at the two bodies — 'these are your pals so you take care of them. Pile them on their horses and start riding. I'm going to be somewhere behind you and if I catch up, then there'll be another grave to dig. Now move.' It took the scared man only a few minutes to tie the bodies across saddles and blubbering his thanks and an assurance that he would never be seen again, headed south and was soon out of sight.

Keeping one eye on the frightened man, Buck watched as Collins calmly replaced a spent shell and shoved his silver revolver back into an underarm holster. You just never knew about a man, he thought.

'Thanks,' Buck said, getting a nod from the buyer in return.

'My boy, I couldn't stand there and let these scoundrels kill someone representing the family of my favorite rancher, now could I? And while we're cleaning out scoundrels, Mr Thompson, you're probably right: it's unlikely that anyone can prove that one of us has been buying shoddy branded cattle, but for some time I have been aware of your purchasing small herds from this siding. As the Rocking C is the largest producer of beef, it would not surprise me to discover, whatever mark they carry, these animals were once wearing that brand. Sir, I would suggest you get on the next train out and not return.'

'But you can't just chase me off.'

'Not only can I, I am,' Collins said, 'On top of that I will make it my business to make sure every rancher up and down the line hears about the buying of obviously stolen cattle. Proving you have shipped such small lots wouldn't be difficult. Now, do you wish to argue with me, sir?' he asked, with one hand still on the pearl-white grips of his holstered pistol.

Wordlessly the other buyer turned and hurriedly made his way to the waiting-room.

'Now, young man.' Collins turned his full attention on Buck. 'I would appreciate knowing what is going on with the Randles and, if you can, some indication as to when I can expect the arrival of the Rocking C herd.'

Quickly Buck told the cattle buyer about the shooting of Virgil and his reason for taking up the fight. It turned out that Collins was an old acquaintance of the professor's. After hearing in more detail how Virgil Randle had died, how dear Matilda was holding up, he stood silent for a minute.

'Young man, I don't know what is going on, but it seems strange to me that it is only the Rocking C cattle that are showing up here. I'd almost think there is someone in Coulter's Landing has it in for the Randles. Also, it is equally perplexing that Virgil would borrow money without Matilda's knowledge; they have always been very close. I don't know anything about the banker Blount but it is typical for bankers, if they are going to remain in commerce, to be a good businessman. Well, give my regards to the widow when you see her. If Professor Fish sent you, I have to believe he knew what he was doing.

When I get to the capitol I'll have a word with the governor about getting the law to this part of the state.'

Making a deal for the herd of young stuff, Buck filled his canteen with fresh water and, slapping the saddle back on his horse, headed back north.

★　★　★

When the sun came up Friday morning, Buck was sitting comfortably on the hotel porch. He had arrived in town well after dark the night before and, after stabling his horse, had taken a room. Now with breakfast out of the way he sat and waited for the rest of the town to come awake. Somewhere in the residential area back behind the stores a rooster crowed his happiness at life. Buck rolled a smoke and watched as a mangy-looking black and white dog, its tail hanging so low it almost trailed in the dust, crossed the street and disappeared under the boardwalk on the other side. He smiled as he looked up to see the butcher's sign over the door there.

Slowly, first this shopkeeper and then that, opened their doors and, some at least, swept the boardwalk in front. It was almost two hours before the hotel clerk came out and handed him two telegrams. The first was from the governor's office and in terse words informed him that at the present time no one was available to come to Coulter's Landing. That brought a frown to Buck's face that the second one, a transfer of $1,200, didn't wipe off. If Matilda held to her decision, the money would simply be transferred back to his bank in Brisby.

He wanted to catch Matilda before she went to the bank to give her the money from the sale of cattle to Collins. Buck wasn't sure what she'd think of that. He'd soon know, though, watching the road into town he saw her wagon coming. Her first stop was at the general store where she entered and a few minutes later came out and turned toward the bank.

Buck met her just as she got to the door and smiling, handed her Collins's money. Explaining where the money came from meant telling her what had happened at the railhead. Looking directly into Buck's eyes, he saw that she wasn't happy with the report, but before she could comment, a horseman rode up and swung down. The two turned to find Hugh Hightower climbing out of his ornate saddle.

'I hope I didn't keep you waiting, Matilda,' he commented, letting his eyes slide to Buck. 'And I hope this friend of yours is not still bothering you.'

'No, Hugh. He brought me some money and information about the rustling.'

'Money? I thought you had agreed to let me take care of that loan.'

Buck stood watching and listening but not commenting, a smile playing on his lips as he saw how unhappy the news made the horse rancher.

'Oh, it isn't enough for this month's payment,' she answered, 'but, well, it does help.'

Not mollified, Hightower was about to comment when the bank's doors opened and two men stepped out. Blount and a well-dressed professional-appearing man.

'Good morning, Matilda,' Blount said, nodding to the men.

'Mrs Randle,' the man murmured. 'Fortunate, my running into you this morning. It'll save me a ride out to your ranch. It is the IOUs left by your late husband I wish to discuss.' This man, Buck saw, was the gambler. Typical of the breed, his worn black suit was clean and recently brushed. Taking in his long, thin face made Buck think of the face of a fox. Everything about the man was thin. A sharp nose separated from thin lips by a well-trimmed mustache had a small knob that indicated it had been broken at least once. His light-brown hair had been recently barbered and was shiny with some kind of pomade. His boots were black and had been polished to a high gleam.

'And this must be the cowboy that showed up to help you. My name is Hubbard, Vance Hubbard,' he said, offering his hand.

Buck shook, feeling the wiry muscular strength under the smooth long-fingered hand. 'James Buckley Armstrong,' he said, 'and I've heard a little about you, too.'

'Yes, well, Mrs Randle, can I count on a visit from you today?'

'First Matilda has some business to take care of with the bank, Hubbard,' Hightower growled. 'That is more important than any questionable IOUs left by her late husband.' Turning to the banker, he motioned toward the door. 'Banker Blount, if you'd be so kind we can get this transaction dealt with.'

Blount opened the door and let Matilda go through first. Hightower followed the banker and, attempting to cut Buck off, reached to close the door behind him. Neither Buck nor Hubbard was going to let that happen and catching the door before it closed, both entered right behind the others.

'You may not approve, Hightower, but the debt left by Virgil Randle must be satisfied.'

'And even a poor cowboy such as myself,' Buck added, with a big smile, 'can have banking business to conduct.'

Without a comment, the banker escorted Matilda and Hightower through the break in the railing, leaving the other men standing outside. Still smiling, Buck strolled over to the single teller window and flattened out the telegram bank transfer. 'I'd like to open an account with this,' he explained.

The teller, a young man wearing a green eyeshade, read the transfer and glancing quickly back at the group gathered at Blount's desk, frowned. 'I'll have to have Mr Blount approve this, sir.'

'Well, then, why don't you just do that?'

'He is busy with other customers at

145

the present time, sir. If you'll just wait?'

'Nope. Can't do that. Tell you what, though. When the good banker is ready for my business you have him find me. I'll be having a cup of coffee in the restaurant.' Turning to Hubbard he extended his hand. 'Hubbard, may I buy you a cup of coffee? There're a couple things I'd like to talk over with you.'

Getting a nod, he led the way out and across the street.

★ ★ ★

'Armstrong, I don't know exactly what your interest in this is, but I don't think it is any of your business.' With cups of strong black coffee steaming on the table in front of the two men, Buck had asked about the IOUs. Hubbard smiled and shook his head. 'This seems to be a matter between the widow Randle and myself. What exactly are you looking for?'

'Well, Mr Hubbard, to tell the truth,

146

I'm fishing. It seems there are a lot of questions floating around but very few answers. The shooting of Matilda's husband is one; the debts that you claim he ran up is another. I'm a friend who is trying to understand how these things happened. Tell me, how did the game that Virgil Randle supposedly lose the money in, go? Who else was at the table?'

Laughing, Hubbard again shook his head no. 'As I said, it's none of your business. All you, as a so-called friend, need to know is that I hold the paper with Randle's signature. And I expect to get my money.'

Buck was saved from trying to come up with another approach by the arrival of Matilda and Hightower. 'Mrs Randle.' The gambler stood and waved a hand invitingly at an empty chair. Without a word of greeting both Matilda and Hightower sat down.

'Buck,' Matilda asked sternly, 'tell Hugh what you told me about the shooting at the railhead.'

'It was simply a case of a coupla rustlers biting off more than they could chew.'

'You seem to have a habit of shooting people and then calling them rustlers,' Hightower frowned. 'What led you to believe these men were really guilty of stealing Rocking C cattle?'

'A matter of brands not matching made it obvious. When they were called on it they made the mistake of trying to shoot their way out of it. Just as the fellow here in town, they were a bit too slow to make it work.'

Hightower glanced at Matilda and grimaced, 'Matilda, I don't think you want to be associated with this kind of man, I really don't. No one has seen any proof that the men he's shot were actually rustlers. And really, since he showed up that's about all he's done, shoot men and call them criminals and, according to one witness, shoot an old man from ambush. You have to get rid of him before he ruins your reputation. People are starting to talk, you know.'

Matilda stared at Buck, waiting for him to respond.

With his usual innocent smile, the big cowboy paused and lifted his cup. 'You know,' he wondered, 'I seem to recall the cattle buyer, Collins, mentioning something. You all know Collins, don't you? After the shooting was over he asked about what was happening with his friends on the Rocking C. I told him what I knew. He hadn't heard about your husband being murdered, Matilda, and sends his sympathies. But he pointed out that it's only Rocking C cattle that have been brought over to the railhead. It seemed strange to him that these rustlers knew which animals to run off. Almost like there was someone here locally telling them. Now that makes me wonder.'

'Makes you wonder? It's clear to me.' Hightower's voice grew loud and demanding. 'You're the stranger here. You're the one shooting so-called rustlers. That is what makes me wonder.'

'Oh, I had a little help along the way. All that shooting wasn't just from me: the cattle buyer, Collins, took a hand in it, too.'

'Buck, are you saying that Mr Collins was there and took your side? Hugh' — Matilda turned to Hightower — 'I've known Mr Collins since, well, since forever. He was one of Pa's friends. If he said those men were rustlers, then I have to believe they were.'

'Mrs Randle, I for one don't care about who shoots rustlers. All I want is to get the money owed to me. Your husband lost at my table and I have the paper he signed to cover his debt. Now, can I have my money?'

'Matilda,' Buck interjected, 'ask him who else was in the game that time. I did, but he didn't want to share any of that with me. Find out who witnessed the game and exactly how the game went. My advice? Don't bother paying it.'

Hubbard scowled and cursed. 'It is a debt and it'll have to be paid by someone. Mrs Randle, I'll give you one week.' Turning abruptly the gambler stalked out.

Hightower glared at Buck. 'I'll stand by what I said, Matilda. This man has no irons in the fire but is acting like he does. You have friends here who care about you. Give it a lot of thought before you follow this man's advice.' Pulling on his hat, he went out the door, slamming it behind him.

Nobody spoke for a while. Buck sipped his coffee and watched Matilda's face as she tried to decide what to do, whom to listen to. 'I just don't know, Buck. I don't know what to do. On top of all this the farmers have let me know there will be no hay or oats this year. Buck, the ranch depends on that to get through the winter. All this is making me sick with worry. Maybe Hugh is right, maybe I need a man to take over and help me run things. I just don't know.'

15

Stopping at the general store, Buck helped the clerk load the boxes and barrels that Matilda had ordered. Once seated and with the reins in hand, she glanced at the big cowboy and shook her head.

'Buck, I think it would be best if you didn't ride with me. Until I can figure out what to do anyway, I think I'll follow Hugh's suggestion. I know,' she added quickly, 'you've been trying to help, but I just can't take any more. Once the herd is sold and I can pay off Hugh and Hubbard I'm sure things will return to the way they were. I'll write to Uncle Fish and tell him you did as good as you could, but . . . ' She let the sentence fade away unfinished.

'If that's what you think is best, well, I can't argue with you.' Touching his hat brim, he smiled up at the woman before walking around to where his horse was tied. Back in the saddle he considered. 'Well, horse, I'd say we've been fired. First time that's happened in a long time,' he muttered, reining about and walking the black back toward the restaurant. It'd been long enough since breakfast to start thinking about lunch.

Sitting in the restaurant waiting for his meal to come, he considered what he could do. He didn't believe the chances of Matilda's world coming back to normal were that good. Somehow, since her husband's death, trouble had been piling up on the young woman. Selling the herd and cleaning up the debts left by the man wouldn't change anything. There was something else going on and he didn't see what he could do about it.

Blowing the steam off a final cup of coffee, he suddenly thought of the old sheepherder. Damn, he thought, I should have seen how he's doing. Leaving a few coins on the table and slapping his hat on, he mounted the black and rode down the street to the doctor's office.

'Nope,' the man coming out of the office door carrying a large cracked leather bag told him, when he asked if the doctor was in, 'I'm on my way out. That Foley woman is about due to add to the family. She is one woman who doesn't believe in wasting time; when she says the baby is coming, its coming.' The doctor's words came as he climbed into a buggy and without glancing at Buck flicked the reins on his horse.

'I'm asking after that sheepherder who was shot.' Buck had to haul around and ride along side the moving buggy.

'Oh, well. He's resting. His boy came and took him a day or so ago. Given lots of rest, he'll be OK. He's a tough old coot. Strong people, those sheep-herders. Go on, Nell.' He snapped the reins on the back of the horse putting it into a gallop as Buck pulled up.

Rather than come into the sheep

camp in the dark, Buck made another dry camp and spent the night quietly watching the stars wheel overhead. Late summer evenings in the high desert country were special. Soon after the sun went down, cool breezes usually came up, spreading the odors left by the day's heat on what plant life there was. Even the cooling rocks added to the evening aroma. Shoveling dirt over his small camp-fire and giving his horse a hatful of water, Buck spread out his bedroll and, lying with his head pillowed by his saddle, he relaxed and watched the sky.

Too early for the moonrise, the sweep of stars was magnificent. In the clear air, the bigger lights looked almost close enough to touch if he only could reach a little further. Far off the call of a coyote brought his attention back to earth and for a while he listened to the night sounds before sleep overtook him.

The sun hadn't reached its highest point when Buck finally reached the Basques' camp. The flock had been moved a little further east and he only had to follow the trail left by the wagon to find the new camp. Stopping in plain view but outside a bit, he called out his hello. Remembering how the young Navarro blamed him for his pa's wound, Buck thought it best to declare his peacefulness.

'Well, come on in.' The return call wasn't strong, obviously from the old man himself.

'Good morning, Mr Navarro,' Buck called, as he rode slowly in to find the old sheepherder lying on a pad of blankets, his back propped up against a wagon wheel. A big smile of welcome greeted the rider.

'And it is a beautiful morning when one can welcome a visitor to his camp. I remember you. You're the rider my son did an injustice to. Making you leave our camp did not show our hospitality. Again, I apologize for that. Will you share a cup of coffee with me?'

Climbing down and ground reining his horse, Buck nodded as the old man pointed to a nearby piece of log. 'Seat yourself. I'm afraid I can't reach the coffee pot and the extra cup, so you'll have to take it. I'm still not moving around too well.'

'I'm damn glad to see you out of that doctor's bed. Just how bad were you hit?'

'Oh, not as bad as it looked. The doctor poked around and discovered that the bullet had torn a big gash but hit a rib and was deflected. He sewed the wound up and here I am, lying in bed while my son takes care of both flocks. A little hot-headed, my boy, but really a good young man.'

'I hope both you and he understand that I had nothing to do with your being shot.'

'From me you have no fear on that score: my son, however, is another matter. He can think of no one other than you, only because you're the last of your kind to be seen anywhere near our camp. I told him that you were a gentleman and was not one to repay our hospitality with such an evil deed,

157

but he is young and does not believe.'

'Has there been trouble between cattlemen and sheepherders before?'

'No.' Sadness filled the old man's face. 'For many years we Basques have held our flocks outside the pastures of both those who raise cattle and horses. We even stay away from the farms that are in the area of the river. This land is not as dry as it looks and our sheep can easily find the feed they need. Until recently there has been no strife.'

Sitting on the log, Buck enjoyed the sheepherder's company as they discussed various things. It was obvious that the old man was happy to have a visitor to spend time with. Finally though, Buck tossed out the dregs of the last cup and, wishing the man well, rode off toward the Rocking C.

★ ★ ★

The early afternoon sun was past its zenith and its intensity wasn't as harsh as he rode into the ranch yard. Not sure of the welcome he could expect, he thought at least he'd get a good ranch meal and a bed for the night, the same any grubline rider could expect. Two other horses were standing hipshot at the hitch rail, one a big proud gray carrying the H Bar H brand. Standing as high as the gray, the other was much broader along the back, and was one of the breeds favored for pulling a farm wagon or plow.

Dropping the reins over the hitch rail, Buck went up the steps on to the veranda just as the front door swung open.

'Buck,' Matilda exclaimed as she saw the big man. 'What are you doing here?'

Following her out the door, Buck recognized the young man who had been standing with the Hightowers after the fight with the blacksmith, Calvin. Taking his hat off, he nodded in answer, 'Why, just riding the grub line, ma'am,' he laughed, thinking he had obviously not been expected. 'Just hoping to get a good meal and a place for my bedroll in your hay barn.' Pointing in the direction of the young man, he said, 'I don't think I've met this man; seen him, but haven't been introduced.'

'I'm Paul Hightower. I know who you are. Everybody knows who you are. What we don't know is why Mrs Randle brought you here.'

'I didn't, Paul. I told you that. A good friend of mine asked him to come help me and here he is.'

'Pa says someone hired him to come in and cause trouble.' The young man ignored Buck.

'Is that what you're doing, Buck? I'm beginning to wonder, especially now. Don't you think you've a lot of nerve, showing up here?' The nervous tension Matilda had shown the last time they'd talked was still evident. 'How much damage are you going to do?'

Noting the solemn looks on the their faces, Buck's smile quickly evaporated. 'What has happened?' he enquired.

'You expect us to think you don't

know?' Paul asked in amazement.

'I don't expect anything from you,' he snapped. Turning to Matilda he asked again, 'What has happened?'

Frown lines masked her face. 'Buck, Vance Hubbard was murdered this morning. Just like Virgil, someone shot him and left him in the road. Hugh and his boys found him and took his body back to town. Buck, the sheriff is saying you're the only one with a reason to kill him.'

16

'I don't think I've ever met so many people so quick to blame me for each and every killing.' Shaking his head disgustedly, Buck walked to the nearest rocking chair and sat down. Whirling his hat in his hands he looked unsmilingly at the pair. 'Now, would someone tell me what this is all about?'

'But you're the last person to talk with him,' Matilda cried out, 'in the restaurant yesterday morning. His bartender told Sheriff Holt that Hubbard came into the saloon and closed his office door and didn't come out until closing time. This morning, they found him lying alongside the road, dead.'

'Paul?' Buck said questioningly. 'Exactly where did you and your pa find Hubbard?'

'Just about where Mr Randle was found. Just left in the dirt next to the roadway. He'd been shot in the chest. A terrible wound, Pa said he had to be dead before he hit the ground. His horse was off a ways chomping at the grass.'

'A terrible wound, you say?'

'Yes.' He grimaced. 'His shirt was all black where the bullet hit him. It looked burnt.'

'So it was more than likely someone he knew and trusted. Probably was riding alongside.'

'We wrapped him in his slicker and took his body back to town. Sheriff Holt said he'd be talking to you about where you were last night and early this morning.'

'Last night? I dry camped a coupla miles from the Navarros sheep camp. I rode in just after daybreak to see how the old man was getting along. We had coffee and a long talk. I suppose it's possible I could have waited for the gambler, shot him and then raced across the valley, but I didn't.' Getting up and jamming his hat firmly in place, he went down the steps and put a foot in a stirrup. 'Well, one problem's been solved,' he said, reining away from the porch.

'What's that?' Matilda asked, despairingly.

'Those IOUs your husband was supposed to have signed: Hubbard can't collect on them now, can he?' Touching the black's side with a spur, he turned away.

Buck didn't get far when he heard his name called. 'Mr Armstrong.' Paul Hightower came running across the yard, catching up.

'Look, maybe what you say is right. Maybe what Pa's been telling us is, well, is what he wants to believe.' His words came fast. 'But in one thing you're right. Matilda has a better reason for not wanting that gambler to come out here. And if she does, then Pa does too. He's determined to help her and he could see that stopping Hubbard is doing just that.' His words ended as Matilda came to stand by him.

'Buck, I apologize for my outburst. It's just that I don't know what's happening,' Matilda's eyes were filling with tears.

'Matilda, I don't know either. So far, the only people I've shot have been two rustlers, and both were given the chance to back up. Both drew against me. Oh.' He remembered the ambush. 'There was the man out on the trail. He and his partners tried to discourage me from heading this way.'

'Did Jose Navarro invite you into his camp?' Paul demanded disbelievingly. 'His son is sure you're the one who shot his dad.'

'Yep. His boy still thinks so, I guess, but Juan doesn't. I didn't run into the boy, he was out with the flock this morning. People' — he raised his right hand — 'I'm not the wild killer that some are saying I am.'

'Mr Armstrong, I guess I want to apologize too. Maybe you're the killer Pa says you are, but I don't know where else to go,' Paul looked away obviously embarrassed. Taking a deep breath he went on, again talking fast, as if trying to get the words out before changing his mind, 'The truth is, I came over here hoping to find you. Everybody is saying you're just a gunman and that you're a killer, but Mrs Randle doesn't think so, and old Navarro must not so maybe they are wrong. It doesn't matter; you're the only one I can think of. I need help.'

Buck settled back in the saddle and grinned. 'First you're sure I'm a killer and then you want my help. Boy, whatever the problem is, it must be something worth listening to. What do you want me to do? Shoot someone?'

'Buck, please listen to him,' Matilda pleaded. 'He came to me for help and you're the only one I could think of. Please.'

'I'm listening.'

'It's my pa. We were riding back to the ranch from town. I heard him tell Frank and Hughie that tonight would be a good time to hit the farmers. He made it sound like a joke. But he's never liked having them in the south end of the basin, says that land shouldn't be plowed. He always thought Miz Randle's pa was wrong to be buying their hay and oats and now with all the trouble you're having, he thinks it's a good time to start moving them out.'

Buck dropped the black's reins and climbed out of the saddle. Facing Paul he frowned, 'Boy, are you telling me your brothers are planning on causing trouble for the farmers? Is this the first time they've done something like this? You know they've been blaming Matilda and her hands. That was what that fight with the blacksmith was all about.'

'I don't know. Pa and my brothers don't talk to me much. Pa always blamed me for my ma's death and my brothers, well, it's always been like I was some poor relation that has to stand outside looking in. But things're different now. I can't let them hurt the farmers.'

'What changed?'

Paul looked for help from Matilda, who stood silent. Finally the young man, head hanging down, whispered, 'Elizabeth Cooder.' Looking up at Buck he pleaded, 'I can't stand by and see her pa's place destroyed just because my pa thinks that land should be used for horses.'

'Buck,' Matilda appealed, 'Paul and Elizabeth have been meeting when they could here at the ranch since early spring. Their fathers would have a fit if they knew, so I let them meet here when they can get away.'

Buck looked first at one and then the other. Shaking his head, he asked, 'Does your pa know where you are right now?'

'No, I'm supposed to be up in the north pasture bringing in a couple of brood mares we keep up there with their colts. But I can't just let it happen, can I?'

'What'll your pa say when he learns you're turning against him? If the farmers are warned, he'll know and it don't take much to figure out you're the only one who could tell them.'

'I don't care,' Paul stood tall, 'I just can't be part of what he thinks is tolerable. Those people have families and are our neighbors. Pa is wrong and Frank and Hughie — they just think it's fun. Will you help?'

'Yeah, I'll go along. But they won't listen to me. Old Cooder in the camp thinks I'm a troublemaker and a killer. One or the other of you will have to go along to convince them to be ready to fight.'

17

While they ate a late lunch of cold beef sandwiches, Matilda told the ranch cook and Freddie she was riding out with Paul and Buck, in case Hank or any of the hands came looking for her. After changing into a soft leather split skirt and long sleeved man's shirt while Buck saddled her horse, she took the lead as they galloped south-east toward the river crossing. Turning away from the road to town, Matilda dropped back to ride alongside Buck and Paul.

'You recall it was Rocking C beeves that had been run into Cooder's fields last time. I wonder if it was the Hightower boys who were behind that? I know Hugh has always wanted to run the farmers out of the basin, but in the past it's always been talk. What would change his mind?'

'Ma'am, I don't want to talk against

my pa, but he really thinks you're going to come around and see things his way. Why, he even made Frank take his spurs off in the house. It won't do, he said, for us to put our feet on the furniture with spurs on if you marry him and come to live at the ranch.'

'Paul, there is no chance of my ever marrying your pa.'

'Paul,' Buck cut into the conversation, 'you said that Hubbard's shirt was scorched by the gunshot that killed him. Matilda, was your husband's shirt scorched?'

'Why, yes. It was one of his new flannel shirts I bought for him on our last trip to Brisby. Where the bullet had gone in, just below his armpit, the shirt was burnt and the skin underneath was black, too. But not burnt, more like it had coal dust rubbed into the skin. I couldn't clean it all. Why?'

'Just wondering. It'd take someone both men knew and trusted to get that close to them. And the gun must have been held close, if the powder caused the shirt to be singed.'

Early dusk came quickly after the sun dropped below the far horizon as they arrived at the Cooder farmhouse; Buck dropped back a bit and looked the place over. The house and barn and the other outbuildings had all been painted recently and were in good repair. A series of small corrals were constructed of wide planks and not poles such as would be found on a cattle ranch. These, he thought, were more likely for milk cows, sheep, pigs and other farm animals. All in all, the farm indicated a lot of ownership pride.

'What do you want?' the old man yelled, stepping out on the porch.

'Good evening, Mr Cooder,' Matilda answered, pulling up in front of the house but not getting down. 'We came over to warn you that someone is planning on running a small herd of my beef across your fields tonight.'

'What? You expect me to believe you when you come riding in with that killer? And what's the Hightower boy got to do with it? I don't trust you, Miz Randle.'

'I understand, Mr Cooder. But we have reason to know what we're talking about. We came together because we knew there isn't one of us you would believe.'

'Mr Cooder,' Buck cut in, 'whether you believe us or not, it wouldn't hurt for you to be ready, would it?'

The farmer stood studying the riders for a minute and then, shaking his head, agreed. 'Yeah. But I don't want any of your help in protecting what's mine. I'll send some of my crew out to patrol near the river and you can be sure, they'll be armed. I told you once, any cattle comes trampling my crops will be shot and I mean it.'

'It isn't my men who'll be behind those cattle. If you have to shoot them to protect your crop, then I'll have to get whoever is driving them to pay.'

'You, boy,' he pointed to Paul. 'What's your take in all this?'

'Mr Cooder, it might be that those

running the livestock into your crops are my older brothers. I think they are wrong and would do the neighborly thing and offer my help, but I'm not going to shoot at my kin, so I will ride on into town.'

Again the older man didn't move for a bit. 'If this is a fact, then I thank you. If it's some kind of game, then you don't need to come riding into my yard again.'

Paul shook his head in denial. 'No, sir, this certainly isn't a game. And once this all gets straightened out, I would like to come calling on your daughter, Elizabeth.'

'Well, if that don't take the cake. You say your brothers are going to try riding over my wheat and then try to tell me you'd like to come courting? Well, I never.'

'Standing here arguing about two young people courting,' Buck smiled in the coming darkness, 'isn't getting anything done. We'll be letting you get on with your work.' Turning his black horse, he led the way out of the yard and down the road toward town.

'I feel real bad,' Paul said, coming up alongside. 'If anyone is hurt or killed tonight, well, they are my brothers.'

'Yeah, I can see how that'd be,' Buck answered understandably. 'But everyone has to make his or her own choices and often the tough part is having to live by them. Something to think about, Paul: everything has a price and the smart man figures the best he can whether he can afford to pay that price. And I don't mean just a horse, a shirt or a pair of spurs. Your actions can be costly too.'

18

It was past dark when the three riders arrived in town. Dropping Matilda off at the hotel, Buck and Paul took the horses to the livery stable and bedded them down for the night. Both men decided that, rather than spend money on a hotel bed, they'd find a pile of hay to dump their bedrolls on.

They were up early the next morning and, after rolling up their bedding and tying them back on their saddles, were washing up at the water trough when the sheriff and a couple of other men came bursting in.

'Hold it right there. Don't you move or we'll fill you full of lead!' the round-faced lawman yelled excitedly. Neither Buck nor Paul had heard them coming up behind and turned around to find the sheriff and the others standing a few feet away covering them with drawn firearms. Sheriff Holt was waving a double-barreled shotgun.

'I knew the first time I saw you, you'd be trouble. Now, I want you to slowly unbuckle your gunbelt and let it drop. You first, stranger.' The shotgun had stopped waving and was now pointed directly at Buck.

'What's this all about, Sheriff?' he asked.

'Don't talk, just do what I said. Drop your gunbelt,' he yelled his answer.

Glancing at Paul, he smiled. 'See how brave your sheriff is? A big shotgun and a coupla friends standing a few feet away and he has to yell at me like I don't understand a word he's saying. He's right, I don't.' Turning back to the armed men, he raised his hands chest-high. 'But I'm not going to get my six-gun all dirty, either. Not until I know what this is all about.'

'Oh, you are the calm one, aren't you. Well, I'll tell you. You are under arrest for holding up the stage. Now, are you going to drop your gun, or do I believe you're going to try to escape. I'd like that a lot.' The shotgun was steady as he brought the stock to his shoulder. 'Paul Hightower, you'd better move away.'

'Sheriff,' Buck said, seeing that Paul didn't move. 'You'd better tell those fellows standing beside you to step aside. I get a notion that your finger is stroking those triggers and I'm liable to start shooting, and we all know how much of a killer I am, don't we?' For a heartbeat nobody moved, and then those close to Holt started inching away.

'Say, Sheriff, where did this robbery take place?' Buck asked, after glancing to the men now standing away from the lawman.

'That don't matter a lick. You were identified by the driver and I'm gonna take you in.'

Paul, still standing close to Buck's side, shook his head. 'When exactly did this stage hold-up take place, Sheriff? I only ask, because I know where this man has been since just after noon yesterday.'

'You just better step away, young man. It don't matter what you say. I tell you he was recognized. Mister, I ain't gonna tell you again, unbuckle your gunbelt.'

'Uh, Sheriff,' one of the other men said softly, 'don't you think you'd better listen to young Hightower?'

'No, damn it! Old Josh Sawyer said this was the man who held a gun on him and by Gawd I gonna take him in.'

'What?' Buck said with surprise. 'You mean this hold-up didn't take place in town? Didn't you tell us that your jurisdiction didn't go past the town's limits? Now I know I'm not going with you. You better think a bit about pointing that shotgun at me, too. I'm getting a mite concerned about that.'

'It don't matter! It was our bank's money that was took!'

Slowly using his thumb, Buck slipped the thong off the hammer of his Colt. 'Sheriff, I won't say it again. Move that shotgun or pull the trigger, 'cause I'm about to get angry.'

19

For the first time, the sheriff saw that he was standing alone. Red-faced he let the shotgun barrels drop until they were pointed at the dirt. 'Damn you! You won't get away with this,' he yelled in frustration.

'That's a lot better,' Buck relaxed his right hand. 'Now, when and where was the stage held up?'

'Late last night, just before dark,' the same man explained. 'Sawyer got to town just before dark and said it'd happened about a mile or so out of town. He came rushing into town, yelling for the sheriff. Said it was a big man riding on a big black horse. That's about all he could see; it was coming on to dusk and the bandit sat his horse in the shadow of a big oak tree.'

'Well, it couldn't have been Buck,' Paul said. 'He and I and Miz Randle were riding together and had left her ranch just after lunch. We left the widow Randle at the hotel after dark and bedded down here in the livery. You can ask Miz Randle and she'll tell you.'

'Seems there is more than one black horse in the area, Sheriff. When you find him, though, I'm sure you'll find he isn't as mean as my black.'

* * *

An hour or so later, Matilda joined Buck and Paul at the restaurant for breakfast. Telling her about the stage hold-up and the charge that Buck was the crook made her decide to add her testimony to that of Paul's before heading back to the ranch.

'Sheriff Holt has an election coming up in the fall,' she explained, 'and it would help him to show how on the job he is. Actually, it's the fact that nobody else wants the job. Having Blount back him makes it easier, I guess.'

The men didn't offer their thoughts,

being busy with flapjacks, fried eggs, thick slices of ham and sourdough biscuits. Matilda watched them put away their big meals after her breakfast of toast and coffee. It was while they were relaxing with coffee and a cigarette that the subject of the planned raid on the Cooder farm was brought up.

'I surely hope my brothers stopped when they saw Elizabeth's pa and his men were waiting for them,' Paul said worriedly. 'They've always been bullies, but I'd hate to find out they caused any harm to the farmers.'

'Makes me wonder what your pa was thinking about, sending his sons on a raid like that.'

'Well, one thing's sure' — Buck, as usual, had taken the chair that faced the front — 'here comes the sheriff, and isn't that Hightower right behind him?'

The three watched as Sheriff Holt came hurrying across the street and into the restaurant. Scowling he made straight for the table.

'Mrs Randle, I suppose by now you've all got your stories straight. I wanted to see you before you met up with these two this morning, but I was late. Are you prepared to swear you were with him,' he said, pointing at Buck, 'yesterday evening?'

'Sheriff, when you wouldn't help me find who killed Virgil I decided I'd work to find someone to run against you in the next election. Your present attitude is not making me change my mind. Yes, the three of us were together all afternoon and until I left them at the hotel late last night.'

Buck smiled coldly. 'Sheriff, you're coming mighty close to accusing us of being liars. Now, that isn't what you meant, is it?' He placed both hands on the table and half rose from his chair.

'No,' he sputtered. 'No, I wasn't saying that at all.'

'Maybe you ought to apologize to the lady, then.' Buck glowered, letting his stance become threatening.

'Apologize for what?' Hightower

interrupted, having come in behind the lawman. 'Apologies be damned, Sheriff. You better have a good reason for not having that gunman in jail. From what Sawyer said, it was pretty clear that this stranger held up the stage and I want to know why he's sitting here, free as a bird.'

'Now, Mr Hightower, I can't arrest him because he has these witnesses who swear he was with them while the hold-up was going on. All Josh saw was a big man on a black horse. That doesn't mean it's this fellow.'

'What? Matilda, what were you doing with him? Didn't I warn you that he's a killer? And what are you doing with them, Paul? You'd better get your butt back to the ranch. This is no business of yours.'

'Hey, Hightower.' Buck had sat back down and now had a friendly smile on his lips. 'Why are you so quick to point me out as a killer? If I were as bad as you're painting me to be, wouldn't it be dangerous for you to rile me?'

'I told you before, I'm only thinking what's best for Matilda, here. You can't deny there've been more shootings since you came to town than ever before. I don't suppose you have someone to tell us where you were when that gambler, Hubbard, was murdered, do you?'

'Actually, I do. Where were you?'

'Me? Hell, why would I shoot him? He wasn't anything to me; I don't gamble. Everybody here in the basin knows me; I belong in this county. Nobody knows anything about you, though, do they?'

Matilda stood up and, pulling on her gloves, looked straight into Hightower's eyes. 'Yes, Hugh, everybody knows you. And they know your two sons, Frank and Hughie. Where were they last night?'

'Frank and Hughie? Why they were moving some stock into the northern pastures. That's where Paul should be today, instead of wasting time sitting here in town. Why are you asking? You don't think they had anything to do with the stage hold-up, do you?'

Buck looked apologetically at Paul and then shook his head. 'Nope, we know they weren't south of town robbing the stage. Although I imagine there's more than one big black horse among your herds. But those boys were, according to what we heard, busy last night over near Cooder's farm.'

Hightower's face went from beet red to gray as the soft spoken words were spoken. Angrily he turned to face Paul. 'Damn you. What'd you tell them? You get back to the ranch right now. I'll take care of you later.'

'I don't think so, Pa. You sent Frank and Hughie and some others to run Rocking C cattle at the Cooders' farm. I don't want anything to do with that and I won't cover for it either.'

Hightower started to lunge at his son and stopped as Matilda stepped in front of him. 'Hugh, I don't know what you were thinking of, but you can't take it out on Paul.'

With both hands curled in hard fists, Hightower stared angrily. 'No son of mine would turn against his family,' he growled between clenched teeth. 'Boy, don't bother coming back to the ranch. I'll have your stuff boxed up and sent to town.'

'Paul,' Matilda smiled, 'there's a job for you at the Rocking C, if you want.' Stepping around Hightower she looked back at the man. 'Honest men are always welcome at my place.'

Laughing at the look on Hightower's face, Buck slapped Paul on the back and, as they both walked past, turned back chuckling. 'Well, Sheriff. Once again it seems like a good idea to wire the governor for a marshal. The crime rate is pretty high, wouldn't you say? Stage hold-up, two citizens murdered and quite possibly some farmer's crops being destroyed. Yes, sir, I'd say there's something very crooked going on around here.'

20

Sheriff Holt and Hightower followed Matilda and the two men out and stood silently on the boardwalk and watched as they rode out of town. Finally with hesitation shading every word, Holt looked up at the other man.

'Is it true, what that hardcase said? Did you send your boys over to stampede Randle cattle on the farmer's crop?'

'Never mind that,' Hightower shrugged. 'Come on, I've got to talk to Blount.' Without another word he strode off down the street. The roly-poly sheriff had to run the first few steps to catch up and then his shorter legs were pumping just to keep up.

'Look, I didn't count on any of this. If that damn cowboy wires the governor for a state marshal we'll all be in trouble.'

'Don't worry about that. You take care of things in town and leave everything else for me to worry about.' Pushing through the double doors of the bank and not looking right or left, Hightower walked straight to the back and without knocking opened Blount's office door and went in. Holt followed a few steps behind.

'Hugh.' The banker was seated behind his big desk, counting piles of bills. Stacks of coins covered the flat top of a nearby writing table. 'I didn't expect you in this morning.' Then seeing the sheriff and the anger on Hightower's face, he stopped counting and motioned toward a chair. 'What's happened? Holt, I thought you were going to hang that hold-up on Armstrong. What the hell happened there?'

'Never mind, Blount,' Hightower grumbled, taking the only other chair in the room. 'That damn Armstrong just happened to be out riding with the Randle woman yesterday. To top it off, my youngest son was with them. We'll have to let that go for a while. But right now, I want you to put more pressure on the widow. Somehow, you have to demand payment of the entire loan.'

'Hugh, I can't do that. Hell, you helped her make last month's payment. There's not much we can do until next month.'

'I had to help her. I wanted to make her more dependent on me. Anyway, if I hadn't have done Armstrong would have, and I couldn't have that. And you can call the loan. She's harboring a killer, and someone who just could have something to do with the rustling. You tell her that she's become a bad risk and you have to call for full payment. Tell her anything, but give her something new to worry about.'

Sheriff Holt had pulled his hat off and was now standing there, holding it by its brim. 'Mr Hightower, we got to be careful. If that Armstrong does wire the governor, Randle's shooting would get looked into and pushing for payment won't look good.'

'Damn it, Holt. I told you, don't

190

worry about any telegram to the governor. Armstrong has already tried that and the governor's office turned him down. Anyway, I'm going to take care of it. He won't be sending any telegrams.'

Blount signaled with one hand, 'Sheriff, why don't you leave us alone. I want to talk to Hugh and you don't want to know what it's all about.'

Looking at the banker and then back at Hightower, Holt frowned. 'There's a lot going on that I don't want to know about. If a marshal does come to town, even if it happened out of town, I'm going to get smeared for not following up on Randle's death. And now there's the shooting of Hubbard. I gotta tell you, I don't like any of this. It ain't what I thought we were doing.'

'Yeah,' Hightower sneered, 'but until now you were right there, doing what you could to make it work. Don't worry so much. You'll still get in on the payoff. Now leave us. Go have a drink or something.'

Both men waited until the sheriff left the room, closing the door quietly behind him before continuing their talk.

'Hugh, he's right. We're doing a lot more than we thought we'd have to do. Now, what's this about your son. Which one was it, Paul?'

'Yeah. He's always been a milk toast. I told Frank and Hughie to drive cattle into the farmer's crop and he heard me. Looks like the little sneak ran to tell Matilda and she told Armstrong. I haven't seen the boys yet, so I don't know what happened.'

'Why, Hugh? You already had the farmers and the sheep-herders against the Rocking C. You didn't need to do anything more.'

'Yeah, I did. That Cooder girl has been riding over to Matilda's to meet with Paul. I couldn't let that go on any more. Those squatters have to go and that's all there is to it.'

'OK. OK. I don't agree, but you're the boss. Now, what's this about Armstrong sending for a marshal. Is that something to worry about?'

'No. I'm going to do what I should have some time ago. Armstrong won't be bothering us any more.'

'We don't know who sent him here, remember. He could have some important friends. I think we should think about having him show up dead.'

'Don't lose any sleep over it. I guarantee he won't show up dead. When I get through, he won't ever show up again.'

21

When they reached the bridge Paul decided he wanted to ride over to see what had happened the night before. Thinking about it, Buck decided he'd ride along. Waving to Matilda the pair turned off and set out at a gallop.

Not sure of the welcome they would get, they pulled up when they came in sight of the farmer's yard and sat in the saddle for a moment. High cloud cover made the day a little cooler than had been and the men had enjoyed the morning ride. Waiting for some sign from the house, Buck once again looked the place over.

'This Cooder takes a lot of pride in his property, doesn't he?' he murmured. 'I guess if your pa thinks the farmer is nothing but a squatter he hasn't seen it.'

'No, Pa wouldn't think of riding over

here. If you don't raise horses or cattle, in his eyes, you just don't belong. Even having the sheepherders on the high desert isn't tolerated. And that country won't support anything else. Pa is kinda blind when it comes to what he thinks is right.'

Finally a man stepped out on the porch and, after staring at the mounted men for a bit, waved them in. If Cooder took satisfaction in his home place, that feeling didn't show up on his person. Where the house, barn and outbuildings were painted and almost new looking, his clothes were patched and worn. Nowhere in the yard could one find any weeds or wild grass growing, but the farmer's hair sprouted in all directions, uncut and uncombed. Emotionless he nodded to the two.

'Might as well step down. If we aren't hospitable this morning it's because we lost a good man last night. Zeke Zimmerman had the next farm over and he and his sons came to help. We heard them coming and before they could reach my fences, we turned them back. In all the shooting and yelling, Zeke caught it. We took his body home this morning. He's got a big family and I don't know what they'll do now. The oldest boy said he can take care of the farm and maybe he will. We'll give him all the help we can and hope for the best, I guess.' If ever Buck had seen a man close to the end of his rope, it was this man.

'Mr Cooder? I'm sorry for that man's death,' Paul's voice was soft.

'Well, that's appreciated. Your warning saved us. I know you said it was your brothers that were behind it all, and I know how much it must have cost you. We are all grateful for your help. It's just too bad that someone has to get killed, that's all.' Cooder stood with his head down for a minute and then looked up at Paul, 'I expect you'd like to see Elizabeth. She's waiting inside. If you don't mind, I'd like to talk with your big friend here.'

Throwing the older man a smile,

Paul was out of the saddle and across the porch just as the door opened. As he disappeared inside, Cooder motioned to Buck to climb out of the saddle.

'Let's walk down to the barn.'

Walking beside the man, Buck saw that he was a head shorter and made even shorter by rarely raising his head. 'You were there to help warn us, and I want to apologize for my talk the last time we met.'

'No reason to say sorry, Mr Cooder. I expect if someone was chousing cattle through my crops, I'd get mad at anybody who ran cattle. But it wasn't the Randles behind your troubles. Hugh Hightower seems to have the opinion that if he's rough enough on you all, you'll pull up and leave. This land, he thinks, should be used to raise livestock, and only livestock.'

'Well, he's wrong. We ain't about to pull up stakes and run. Even if we did, there're others who'd come in. This is good land for dry farming. But that isn't what I wanted to talk about. It's about that boy, Paul. My Lizzie has been railing me ragged about him. What do you think of him?'

'I don't know much about him, but Matilda Randle seems to think highly of him. He made it clear that he wanted to come warn your people after hearing his pa tell his brothers what to do. I guess that makes it clear that he has strong feelings for your daughter.'

'That must have been hard for him, coming here to tell us about his brothers' plan. How will he take it when he finds out that one of them got shot?'

Buck stopped and looked down at the man. 'Ah, well now. That could change things, couldn't it?' Looking back over the yard, he considered. 'I don't know. We talked a bit about how hard it is to make a decision, but I doubt if he took into account anything like that happening. I just don't know how he'll take the news. How bad was his brother hit?'

'I didn't see it happen and don't know. One of the hands bragged about knocking one of the leaders out of the saddle, but later, after they turned and ran for it, we didn't find anything. It had to be one of the brothers, though.'

'He'll have to know. This morning, when his pa heard that Paul had been with me, he got damn mad. Hightower told Paul not to bother going back to their ranch. Matilda Randle said she'd give him a job and somewhere to stay.'

'I don't know what's happening. Ever since me and Ma came here, it's been a good life. We raise our wheat and crops and keep to ourselves. Now, well, things have changed and I fear they're gonna get worse before they get better.'

★ ★ ★

Paul must have been told about one of his brothers being shot by someone in the house. Riding with Buck back to the Rocking C later, he was quiet until they reached the turn off.

199

'I guess I'd better head on back to our ranch. I got to know what happened last night, if it was Frank or Hughie that got shot.' He was miserable in the decision.

'Do you think your pa is going to welcome you if one of his boys was hurt by the farmers? Don't forget how he took the news that you'd been with Matilda and me in warning the farmers. I'd think this over real carefully, Paul,' he warned.

'I don't know what to do.' Glancing over at Buck, he asked the big man what he'd do.

'I can't rightly say, boy. It seems to me foolhardy to go riding in if Frank or Hughie has been shot. But I can see how you'd want to know. Maybe you ought to talk to Matilda about it. She might have heard something.'

'Yeah,' Paul quickly decided. 'Maybe she can tell me which way I should jump. I just don't know.'

'There seems to be a lot of that going around. Come on, let's ride on in and see what's what.'

Matilda was sitting on the porch when they rode in. Even before getting down off his horse, Paul was asking about his brothers.

'I don't know, Paul,' she replied, showing her distress. 'All I've heard is that some twenty or so head of our stock had been pushed down in the south end and were grazing peacefully this morning. Hank and some of the boys had heard the shooting late last night and he sent someone down to see what it was all about this morning. He didn't say anything about seeing any sign of what the critters were doing, but being that far south now could mean only one thing. They've all been brought back toward the holding ground.'

'That means I'll have to ride over to find out myself.'

'I wouldn't, Paul. Your father made it real clear that he didn't want you around. I'd wait and let him cool off some before I went riding in over there.

If either of the boys got shot, we'll hear about it soon enough, I reckon.'

It didn't take much more than that to talk him into staying clear of the H Bar H. Matilda made it easier by sending him out to the holding ground and putting him to work on the round-up gather. After he threw his saddle on to a fresh horse, Buck watched him ride out.

'I didn't want to say it in front of the boy, but there was a hat found down by the river. It was all bloody, but none of the men could say who it belonged to.'

'Maybe I should ride down that way, see what I can find out. If nothing else I could use another sack of tobacco. If one of Hightower's boys got shot up, the news is sure to be a major topic in town.'

Matilda frowned. 'Is that a smart thing to do, going into town? Sheriff Holt is certain to still be upset and if anyone on that stage has been talking there'll be others in town who will believe you're the robber.'

Buck laughed. 'Yeah and my riding in

will either convince them I'm truly bad or show them that I couldn't be guilty. It's probably a good idea to show my face around a little more. Likely someone'll get nervous and make a mistake. Something's going on, like I said before, and I want to know what it is.'

'Well, you be very careful. I wouldn't like to find your body lying alongside the trail somewhere.'

'Now, Mrs Randle, I do think you're starting to believe I'm not the killer bad guy you thought I was not so long ago.'

The young woman's face flushed and she quickly rose from the rocking chair and went to the front door. Opening it she turned and once again looked at Buck. 'That was when I'd been listening to Hugh. Now we see where he stands. A girl can change her mind, can't she?' she asked, going in the house.

22

Taking his time, he stopped to water his horse at the river before crossing the bridge. Sitting quietly alongside the fast moving water, he again watched the flows around rocks and over a nearby gravel bar. If that pool behind those boulders out in mid-stream wasn't home to a big, hungry trout, then he'd eat his hat. Even as he watched, the surface dimpled as some sort of winged insect tried to swim its way to safety. Just that little movement and the insect had become supper for the unseen trout.

Smiling at the action, Buck wasn't aware he had company until he heard the harsh command from behind him.

'Move and I'll kill you.' Slowly he twisted around to find both Hugh and Frank Hightower sitting their horses, both pointing Winchesters at his back.

'Now very slowly, unbuckle your gunbelt and toss it back here,' Hugh ordered.

Buck hesitated, but could see no way out of his predicament so he did as he was told, wrapping the belt as tightly around the holster to protect the weapon as much as possible. He needn't have worried. Frank had dismounted and caught the heavy belt before it hit the rocks.

'Now this is what I call a real prize,' Hugh laughed, 'finding you alone with nobody within miles, just sitting there like a Christmas present. Frank,' he said, without taking his eyes off Armstrong, 'take those pigging strings you carry in your saddle-bags and tie his hands to his saddle horn. Be careful and don't get between us. Don't trust him any.'

Frank did as his pa told him, wrapping the thin leather thongs tightly around each wrist and then securing them to the saddle. 'I don't think you'll be using those hands for a while.' Like his pa, the young Hightower's laugh held little humor. The thin cords were already cutting into the circulation. Buck knew that soon his hands would become discolored. He faced his tormentor and didn't let anything show on his face.

'Big, brave gunman, ain't you?' Hugh said, kneeing his horse close and taking the black stud's reins. 'Well, we'll see. Yes, we'll see just how brave you are.'

Hugh headed out, leading Buck's horse with Frank bringing up the rear. Turning away from the road after crossing the river, the three rode west in single file, keeping to the trees and willows that bordered the water. Keeping an eye on the sun, Buck figured they had been riding for three hours or so after leaving the river before Hugh changed direction. Leaving the river they were crossing what Juan Navarro had called the high desert. The rolling landscape was covered with juniper trees, clusters of sagebrush and sparse clumps of sun-dried grass as far as the eye could see. Ahead in the direction Hugh was now taking, all Buck could see was the snag of a long-dead tree standing alone on the top of a slight rise.

'This will do, boy.' Hightower motioned to his son. Frank laughed and got down from his horse. Patting the black on its rump, he came alongside Buck and, taking a Barlow folding knife from a hip pocket, open the big blade and cut the pigging string. Pain shot through Buck's wrists and arms as the blood flowed once more. Grabbing Buck's leg, he was lifted and thrown out of the saddle. Surprised, he tried to twist so he'd land on his shoulder, but was only partially successful.

Still chuckling, Frank took the reins of all three horses and tied them to a low branch of a juniper tree. Buck, lying flat on his back with the wind knocked out of him, grimaced as the blood reached his fingers causing them to tingle painfully.

'You comfortable?' Hugh chuckled.

He reached down and, taking hold of Buck's arm, lifted him. Still feeling the effects of being dumped off his horse and not being able to use his hands, Buck was unable to resist. 'Give me a hand here, boy,' he called to Frank. Together they lifted the cowboy and leaned him against the dried tree trunk. Pulling one arm out, Hugh quickly tied Buck's left wrist to a leafless snag of a limb as Frank tied his other arm to a limb on the other side. Both men stepped back and looked over their handiwork.

'Now you see how it is, killer?' Hugh snarled. 'You've been causing me a lot of trouble since you come into the basin, but that's over now. Your warning those damn squatters cost me a son. I'll take care of them, but now we've got you to deal with. And that's what we're going to do, right Frank? I got to warn you, Armstrong. My boy here is damn mad about losing his brother. I'll protect you, though. I won't let him kill you.' His chuckle was without humor.

Buck had been watching the two men's faces as Hightower made his speech and could see that nothing he said would have any impact so he kept silent. Frank was only a little shorter than his pa's six feet but he looked to be a little heavier. Knowing he had nothing to lose, he smiled. 'Boy, sorry to hear about your brother. It was probably a bad idea, your trying to do those farmers damage. Like I've said, everything has a price and it looks like your brother paid in full.'

'Damn you,' Frank roared, stepping in and hitting Buck in the stomach, folding him over. Hanging from his bound wrists, he tried to regain his feet when another blow landed on the side of his head.

'Frank,' Buck heard the elder Hightower call to his son through the ringing in his ears, 'if you're going to do that, you'd better put on gloves or you'll hurt your hands.'

The leather gloves tore at Buck's face as the young Hightower slapped him, first one side and then the other. Grunting with his effort, Frank threw one fist after another into Buck's unprotected stomach, missing the soft middle once or twice to land his blows on one side of the rib cage or the other. Blackness hovered as the bound man's vision narrowed. Fist after fist tore skin from both cheeks as the young man punished the man tied helplessly to the tree. Gratefully the pain grew fainter as Buck finally lost consciousness, his world fading out to complete darkness.

23

Awareness returned with sharp pain shooting through his arms. Coming awake he found his hands once more tied too tightly to the saddle horn. When he tried to move his legs, he discovered his legs had been tied to the saddle's stirrup leathers. The sun beat down on his head like a drum.

'Hey, Pa, he's awake,' Frank yelled out, somewhere behind him.

'Good. It's no good if he doesn't know what's going to happen to him.' Dropping back to ride beside Buck, Hightower smiled evilly. 'Too bad about losing your hat. That sun'll cook your brains if you don't keep your head covered. But that's the least of your worries. Do you know where you are? I doubt it. Being a stranger in this part of the state, you wouldn't know about the big sand blow, would you?'

Buck didn't have the strength to answer, wasn't even able to raise his head to look around. The pain from his wrists and arms was sharp agony almost overshadowing the dull pain of his face. Almost. That hurt, combined with the soreness of his stomach made him wonder how long Frank had pounded on him.

'You see, the sand blow starts way up north and spreads out as you travel south. Of course, a smart man wouldn't travel anywhere near this desert because there isn't any water. None anywhere. Now, you being a stranger wouldn't know that so when somebody finds you, if anybody ever does, it'll just be your bones that're found. No hat, no water and soon, no horse. Just another case of your taking the wrong turn and getting lost. Too bad, don't you think?'

'Pa, that horse of his looks to be a good one. Ain't there some way we could mix him in our herd?'

'No, I don't think so, Frank. What we'll do is take the stallion back and let him run loose. Someone'll find him and when we hear about the lucky guy finding a big black with a brand no one recognizes, we'll offer to buy him. I agree, he'll make a good addition to our stock.'

Without raising his head, Buck tried to make out where they were. Looking sideways all he could see was sand dunes undulating into the distance. Feeling the pain from the bright sun scorching his eyeballs, he quickly closed them and relaxed to the jogging of his horse, the throbbing in his head matching the jolting of his head.

★ ★ ★

The next time Buck returned to consciousness was when the three stopped. Only partially aware, he felt his hands being cut loose. The sharp stabbing pain took his attention and he didn't know that his legs had been loosened also. Not until, like the first time, his leg was jerked up and he was thrown from the saddle. This time he landed flat on his back in soft, gritty sand. Hot sand.

'Well, Mr Armstrong, this is where we leave you. When you look around I think you'll agree it's a good place. At least as good as any. From where I sit they all look alike. Just sand as far as I can see. No water, just sand and the sun,' his laugh sounded harsh. Frank rolled Buck over, tightening the gunbelt around his waist. 'There. Now when someone finds your body they won't wonder why you weren't wearing your six-gun. C'mon Frank. We got a good ride ahead of us to water.' Laughing the two rode away, leading Buck's big black stud.

This time it was the cool air that brought the big man back to life. Buck faintly remembered hearing the Hightowers' laughter before passing out. Waking up shivering, he curled up and clutched his swollen hands to his stomach. Time passed as he slowly became aware of where he was. Except for the light breeze that blew across the sand there was only one other sound, that of his groans as he sat up. Leaning forward with his elbows on his knees he thought about what had happened. They had beaten him and then left him to die. Somehow he had to beat that.

Resting with his head hanging, Buck tried to think. How long had they ridden after the beating? How far into the sand blow had they came before dumping him off his big black? More importantly, he realized, which direction did they go when they rode off?

His head still ached with each beat of his heart and each time he moved his skin, stiff with dried blood, felt like it was being ripped off. But he had to start if he was going to survive. To sit through the coolness of the night was to die in tomorrow's heat. The swelling from the beating his face had taken had left his cheeks puffed up and he could barely open his eyes. Seeing through thin slits, he looked around sluggishly. The moon, having just risen above the dark horizon, lit the landscape and let him see the stark sameness. Clumps of low-lying brush were few and far between, each throwing long shadows across the blowing sand.

Letting his head drop, he rested with his chin on his chest and thought about a drink of cold water. Chasing that thought out of his mind, he took a deep breath only to be stopped by pain. Breathing deeply expanded his chest and sent pains through his upper body. Frank had hammered him and now every one of those wallops offered its own level of pain. It was quite possible, he realized, that he had one or more cracked ribs.

Forcing his eyes open, he looked down and saw the marks left in the soft sand where he had lain. Looking up a little, he found where the soft blowing sand was filling the depressions left by the walking horses. That way, he saw, was where he'd have to go. Toward that bush near the top of the next dune. He'd have to crawl, but he couldn't just sit here and die.

Crawl he did. Standing up was impossible. The pain in his stomach nearly made him faint when he tried to straighten up. To move at all meant going on hands and knees and his hands were still too painful to support his weight. On his elbows and knees was slow, but he did move toward that bush.

Reaching his goal he went on the few feet to the top of the low dune and, with the moon rising directly behind him, he sighted ahead for the next goal. Hour after hour he crawled. As the feet and yards went by he found his body loosening and he was able to maintain a certain rhythm . . . one elbow to pull and a knee to push and then the other side. The trail he was leaving in the sand, he thought, was probably a lot like that left by the movement of a sidewinder rattlesnake.

Exhaustion finally caused him to stop and rest. The moon, early in its monthly phase, was almost directly overhead as he simply ceased all movement and let his head droop. Tired and sore as he was, he realized that he couldn't surrender to sleep. Some time before the moon set he'd have to find a place to hole up. Some place with a little shade to protect him from the sun that was sure to make the next day painful. A place next to a waterhole would be asking too much, he smiled . . . or tried to smile. Even that made his face hurt. Between his torn skin and the dryness of his mouth, any smiling would have to wait.

Rested, he started out again. Up this dune, down the other side, sometimes letting his weight overbalance him and he'd roll down the next slope, crawling on to his next goal to do it all over again. He had no way of telling how far he went but he had to keep moving. The realization that he couldn't even be sure he was still going in the right direction was almost too much. Shaking his head in denial, he forced that thought away. No matter. He'd have to keep moving.

Luck was with him. Coming to the top of an especially tall dune, he started looking ahead for his next marker when he noticed that darkness was thinning out. False dawn, a sign that the sun would be coming up in a few minutes. For a while he'd been aware that clear thinking had become more difficult. Tiredness and loss of moisture made his head feel like it was full of soft cotton. Getting a thought through that thick mass was becoming harder as the night wore on. Sluggishly, he mulled over whether to stay on top of the dune or to roll to the bottom. The question of where would be a better place to spend the coming day seemed to take a long time to frame. The answer took even longer.

He was about to just let gravity take control when he noticed that the down side of the dune he was on didn't just slope off. He was on top of some kind of low bluff. He'd have to circle around a ways. Out of habit he spotted the next goal, a strange-shaped bush, and rolled to one side. Crawling a little and rolling, letting the loose sand help, he finally made it past the side of the bluff and slid to the bottom. Now he could see what had got in his way. It was a rock outcropping. In the waning moonlight, the low lying wall of shale-like rock was in darkness. Lying still, resting his tired body, he watched as the light of the coming dawn showed him one corner was darker than the rest. He'd found a small overhang. This might offer him some shelter from the coming day's heat.

24

The overhang wasn't enough to keep his entire big frame out of the sun but without it he'd not have made it through the day. The shade, with the exception of the earliest hours of the day, was enough to keep his head and upper body out of the direct blistering sun. Moving as the sun made its gradual way across the bright blue sky, he was able to keep everything protected except his legs. By noon his feet, inside the leather boots, felt like they were cooking. Try as he might, he couldn't curl enough of his body to get all the way under the narrow rocky cave.

Late afternoon, when the sun pasted its zenith and shade from the rock outcropping itself began shading the bottom of the shallow gully, the difference was remarkable. Battling the heat and working his hands helped keep Buck from dwelling on his growing thirst. He couldn't remember the last time he'd had a drink. Thinking about it made his dry mouth water, early on. Later in the morning he slipped a small round rock under his tongue, hoping to generate saliva. But by the time the life-saving shade began its slow march across his broiled legs, his tongue had swollen and even if he could have closed his mouth, his lips wouldn't have met around it. Blisters around his lips had cracked and even that little amount of moisture drained away because his tongue wasn't able to move.

Lying still in the afternoon shade he thought about the coming night. Somehow he'd have to find water; he knew he wouldn't last another day without it. It seemed, lying still to conserve his strength and possibly reduce the amount of sweating, he could feel his body dry out. Late in the day, just before the evening breeze sprang up, he realized he was no longer sweating: that was a bad sign.

It was hard, outwaiting the sun, wanting to begin the night's journey to either water or death, but he knew outside the gully the sun was still burning the sand. Move or die, his mind told him, move or die. But move too soon also meant death. The breeze and shade made a noticeable drop in the temperature, though, and moving slowly and carefully, and using the rock wall for support, he stood up. Weakness made his legs tremble and without the rocks behind him he would have fallen over. Tonight, he swore, he wouldn't crawl, he'd walk.

Even without water, the day's rest had refreshed him. At first his steps were shaky and more of a shuffle than a real step, but as the moon, a little larger tonight, came up, his muscles worked loose and his stride lengthened. Before the full light of the big, yellow white orb began shortening the shadows of rocks and bushes, he was making good time. At least now he was walking up the dunes, going from one clump of sagebrush or rock to another. The first target he saw, the odd-shaped bush he'd marked in his mind that morning, had turned out to be a large rock. More and more as he made his way, rocks and even a few boulders started showing up.

As he walked, keeping his mind focused on maintaining what he hoped was the right direction, he flexed his hands. Trying not to think of how thirsty he was he built a mental image of what he must look like, his face streaked with dried blood from the beating or blistering from the sun-burned area that were more usually protected by his wide hat brim. Those thoughts helped for a while but as his body began to tire the throbbing of his head and the other pains that filled his body became minor. Thirst filled his every thought.

As his legs fought to keep moving, his vision began to blur. Standing for a minute on the slight rise that had taken a long time to climb, he looked ahead.

Where last night he had been looking through mere slits, now he could open one eye fully and the other, still blocked by a rough-feeling scab, would only open about halfway. But there, just a head a ways was a shimmering pond of water. Yes, there. Excitedly he took off running, only to fall as he tripped over a bush.

Groaning and with new soreness, he slowly got to his feet and looked for the pond. Disappointment filled him as he saw nothing but more sand, brush and rocks for as far as he could see.

Drunkenly now, he walked as his legs felt close to giving way. He wanted a drink. He wanted to lie down and sleep. Why not? Wouldn't it be easier if he just lay down for a while? Get some rest and then go on?

No. Images of Hightower laughing as he rode away filled his mind. No. He wouldn't give up. There was an accounting coming and by damn he was going to be there to get his due. For another hour or two he walked, going from one rock to the next, from one goal to the next, heading for water.

Breathing through his nose was becoming difficult. His tongue seemed to fill his mouth and for a time he'd been breathing through his nose. Now trying to fill his lungs with the cool night air was taking real concentration. His whole head felt like it was thick and full. One step at a time, with wobbly, trembling legs he walked through the moonlit night. Earlier he had walked without stopping. After a few hours it was too much and he had to stop and rest. As the moon moved across the sky his rest stops came more frequently. Looking ahead for the next goal he saw that the moon was nearing the far horizon. Daylight wouldn't be far away.

He couldn't stop. Even if he found another rocky overhang to cower in, he'd never make it through another day without water. He couldn't stop. Weaving, stumbling and more than half asleep, he went on. Now, as the morning sun started bringing light to his world, he no longer was looking for the next marker to walk toward, he just walked.

Buck didn't know when he fell, he was unconscious before hitting the ground. As the sun came up and the heat of the day fired up he wasn't aware of it. Even with the bright light of day shining fully on him, he didn't move.

25

For a long time there was nothing but brightness. His world was no more than a glaring intense unmoving brightness that would gradually fade away into black nothingness. Once, when coming up into the bright shimmering he thought he could see a gray shadow moving by. Trying to figure out what this was, he gave up and once again let go and let the thinking grow fainter as he slipped into unconsciousness.

A cool wet cloth pressing lightly against his lips brought him by easy stages to awareness. Feeling weightless, he tried to open his eyes but couldn't. Comfortable coolness made him accept his stillness. Hazy, he could hear voices far away. Not wanting to move he fell back to sleep.

It was the movement of light and shadow playing on his eyelids that woke him up. Opening one eye, he saw a dirty white canvas tunnel curved overhead. The dark skeleton shadow of a tree limb swaying played on the other side. His world exploded into bright sunlight as a canvas curtain was flung back at the end of the tunnel.

'Well, so you finally decided to wake up and join the living, huh?' The man climbing into the tunnel was a dark shadow with the sunlight behind him. 'You are alive, aren't you?' Buck tried to figure out where he was. The last thing he remembered was intolerable thirst, a pain-filled world and putting one foot ahead of the other. Turning his head to see where he was, brought a groan and a stab of fire.

'Ah, well, I would not be moving around too much too soon, young man. Somehow you've gotten yourself in trouble and it'll be a while before you are completely out of it. Now, rest and in a little while I'll have food brought to you.' Softly chuckling the man turned and, moving very carefully, climbed down. It was Juan Navarro. That meant the tunnel was more than likely the sheepherder's wagon. Wondering how that came to be, he dozed off.

Hunger and the smell of coffee roused him the next time. For the first time the dull ache in his stomach was hunger, not from the beating he'd taken. Moving very slowly and carefully, he pulled the thin blanket away from him and tried to sit up. Wearing only his long johns, he looked down to see that his upper body was a mass of greenish-tinged black and blue blotches. Moving even that little bit caused each one to throb.

Getting out of the bed and making his way to the end of the wagon took a long time, but the smell of cooking food helped him along. Pushing aside the curtain he looked out on the sheepherder's camp. The old Basque sat on a blanket, leaning back against a log on one side of the cook fire. He looked up when Buck stuck his head out. His son, Jose, had been stirring something in a big fire-blackened pot hanging over the fire but now stared up at the man crawling out of the back of the wagon.

'Here,' Juan cried, motioning to his son, 'help him, Jose.' The young man didn't move and Buck stumbled over and lowered himself to the ground, leaning back against the log with a sigh.

Glowering at the young man, Juan commented, 'You should probably stay lying down for a while longer.' His son said nothing but went back to stirring the pot.

'I couldn't stand it,' Buck's voice sounded more like a frog croaking than his normal gruffness. 'The smell of food caused my stomach to raise such a noise that I couldn't sleep any more. I don't know how long I've been lying around, but I'll be surprised if my belt still fits.'

'I guess a cup of coffee would be the place to start. Since we brought you in, you've been drinking nothing but water. No wonder you're hungry.' Pouring a cup he handed it across to Buck. Gratefully, the big man sipped the hot liquid and nearly dropped the cup.

'Yes, your lips are still a bit raw. I should have warned you.'

'Raw lips and from what my chest looks like, a face that is one big blister, I'd say. You're moving around a bit more since the last time I saw you. How's that wound coming along?'

'Ah, it takes an old man longer to heal. Slowly, yes, slowly I am getting better. Thankfully, for all his bad manners, my son is making things better for me. On the other side, you look a lot worse and move like you hurt a lot more, but, no, you are not as bad as one would expect. Losing your hat out in that sun wasn't a good idea. But from the marks on your body I have a feeling you didn't just lose your way or your hat.' Juan didn't ask questions outright, but it was clear he wanted to know.

'It certainly wasn't my idea of a good way to see more of your country. How did you find me?'

'It was Jose who found you. First he

found your horse and then when he went looking for you, thinking you'd maybe fallen off or been bucked off or something, he found you. You were unconscious and looked dead but let out a groan when he tried to turn you over. He put you on your horse and brought you here to camp. That was three days ago. We've been giving you a little water every so often.'

'Well, I owe you my life, Jose. I don't know how far I came or how long I was without water, but I don't think I'd have made it another day.' Jose didn't respond. Tapping the big spoon on the side of the pot, he sat back from the fire and watched Buck.

His father frowned at the young man's discourtesy and glanced at Buck. 'If you don't mind my asking, how did you get in such a state? It looks like you've been in a big fight and didn't do so good.'

'I let a couple of hard men get the drop on me,' he explained, and went on to tell about the beating and the ride out into the sand blow. As he talked, Jose's attitude began to change. 'That's where I got to, where you found me, Jose,' he finished his story.

'They tied you up and then beat you? And then took you out into the sand blow without your hat or water?' Jose was sitting up now, asking his questions with unbelieving bluntness. 'Why would they do that? They are one of the old families here in the basin. All you people have always stuck together. Why would they turn against you like that?'

'I can only guess what Hightower is thinking, but his reason for the beating and leaving me to die out there is probably because his son, Hughie, was shot by a group of farmers. You can't put all the cattle ranchers and horse breeders together and say they are all alike. No more than anyone can lump all the farmers or the sheepherders together.'

Juan laughed softly. 'I've tried to tell him that but he would not believe. Now,' he went on, turning to his son, 'with the evidence in front of you, maybe you will open your eyes and your mind and begin to see.'

'Hey, this is the young man who saved my life. Don't be too hard on him,' Buck smiled, only to wince as his lips cracked.

'Ah, you need more salve. I have been putting a lot of special salve on your bruises and cuts. It is a mixture that makes things heal quicker. Your face and hands were very sunburnt but this salve takes that away very fast.'

Smelling his hands, Buck frowned. 'It smells like something I can't quite identify. Familiar but somehow strange smelling.'

His words brought more laughter from the old sheepherder. 'Yes, to you it would be a different smell. The salve is made with the oil from the sheep's wool. So you will smell like a sheepherder for a while,' he laughed.

Jose didn't join in but continued to stare into the fire with a serious look on his face. 'Tell me,' he finally asked, looking across at Buck, 'if what you say is true, that the horse rancher Hightower beat you up and left you to die out in the blow, and he was behind the damage to the farmer's crops, then it might be that he was the one who shot my father. Does that make sense to you?'

'No, it doesn't make sense, but, yes, it's likely he is behind all those things.'

'Then my father is right. I have not been treating you as I should. I offer my apologies and welcome you to our home.' A bare smile crossed his face with his stiff and stilted words.

'So, my friend,' the old man smiled, 'there is at least one goodness to come from your pain: my son learns a lesson.'

★   ★   ★

For the next four or five days Buck Armstrong rested and, feasting on the delicious meals that Jose cooked in the big pot, regained his strength. Each day as he and the old sheepherder sat by the fire, drinking coffee or, more often, cup after cup of strong black tea, they discussed a variety of topics. All the time Buck worked at flexing his hands and, during the last day or so, his legs and back. Slowly the pain faded and, by the end of a week in the sheep camp, was mostly just a bad memory. Only the recollection of thirst still disturbed his sleep.

Each day, Jose walked the flock out in a different direction from the camp. Once, before starting the morning fire, he hitched up the wagon and with Buck and his father sitting inside and the big black horse tied to the tail gate, moved the camp a few miles.

At the end of the fifth day, after yet another delicious stew of mutton, potatoes and strange smelling spices, Buck told the herders that he'd be riding out early the next morning.

'Yes, I have been watching as you prepared yourself. Still you must take care. Although your face has a good start to heal, it could frighten any innocent young person,' Juan joked. This time even Jose joined in with a chuckle. 'Seriously though, you must take care. The men who did this to you will not take kindly having you turn up again.'

Buck's smile lost its humor and became hard. 'I'm counting on that. My showing up ready to collect on the debt will be my little surprise.'

The sun was barely up when he saddled the black and swung up. Once again thanking the Basque herders for their hospitality, he gigged his horse into a brisk walk and headed to the Rocking C ranch house.

'Let's see what kind of welcome the good Widow Randle will have for us, old boy.' As usual the black horse didn't react to the soft spoken words.

26

'Buck!' she hollered, catching sight of him riding into the ranch yard a few hours later. Running to him, she threw her arms around him as he climbed out of the saddle. 'They said you were dead.' She blushed, dropping her arms and looking his face over. 'What happened to you? Are you OK?' The questions came fast and furious as, taking his arm she pulled him up to the porch.

'Hugh came over once a week or so ago, and said he'd heard your horse had been found out near the big sand blow. He thought you'd probably thought you could ride across and ran into trouble.'

Laughing at her excitement, he nodded. 'Well, part of that is true. I was out in that sandy piece of hell and I did run into trouble. As far as finding my horse? No. Jose Navarro found it. Jose found me, too, and saved my life.'

'Tell me all about it.'

Sitting in the rocking chairs, he told her what had happened. How Hugh and his son had beat him up and left him out in the desert and how the Navarros had helped him back to health. He didn't mention the pain and suffering, thinking to spare her.

'Buck, I've been out there and I've seen what happens when someone dies out there. I know what a full day in that sun would do. You're darn lucky to be alive.'

'Well, I couldn't just go away without saying a word to you, now could I?' he smiled. 'Anyway, I don't think your friend should get away with making me lose my best hat. Which reminds me, I think I'll ride on into town and take care of that little business.'

'When Hugh came out, he was riding with Mr Blount, the banker. It appears that the bank, which is Blount,' she said disgustedly, 'has decided that the loan has to be paid in full right now. The reason he gave was that you had become a part of the picture and, as a suspected killer and stage robber, the bank couldn't allow the loan to continue.'

'Now that doesn't surprise me. How long did they give you?'

'Oh, I simply stood up, walked right up to that self-righteous fool and told him to suck eggs. According to Hugh, the big bad killer was gone so there was no cause for him to call in the loan. He huffed and blustered a little but finally turned his buggy around and left. I had to laugh, which didn't please Hugh very much. He warned me again that I didn't know what I was doing, that I needed a strong man to help me run the ranch. I couldn't help it, I laughed at that too. He cursed and rode out. I felt sorry for his horse, he jabbed his spurs into the poor beast's sides pretty hard.'

Buck laughed. 'Well, I guess we'll just have to stick a spoke in Mr Hightower's wagon. I don't think he'll expect me to show up. Now, what's the chance of this poor old grubline rider getting a bite to eat?'

'Oh, you poor old man. You are in luck today. Both Cookie and Freddie have gone out to the holding ground with the chuck wagon. Hank and the hands are starting the drive in the morning. That means for the next couple of weeks any cooking done here will come out of my kitchen.'

Laughing, he followed her through the house and out into the sun-filled kitchen. 'As long as there's no mutton in the pot, I'll be happy. That's about all the Navarros fed me. Pot after pot of one kind of mutton stew after another. I think that's about all they eat.'

'Well, you're not in a sheep camp now. This is cattle country so you'll get a nice big steak.'

★   ★   ★

It was hard to leave the ranch a couple of hours later. Maybe, he thought as he

242

tightened the cinches and, with a wave, rode out, there's been too much lying around lately. 'You don't think we're getting lazy, do you?' he asked. Patting the thick neck he warned, 'That means you, too, you know. Don't think that hanging around a sheep camp doing nothing for a few days is going to become a habit. No, I expect we'll have to run a little of that sluggishness out of your system.' Getting no response, he nodded. 'Maybe later.'

The afternoon sun was starting to lose its heat but Buck nonetheless felt the heat. That feeling might be more of a memory of his days and nights in sweltering temperatures out in the desert, but he still found himself reining the black toward the shady side of the road when possible. Just like his almost unquenchable thirst, it just wouldn't go away. When he thought about his recent experience, however, he felt a great joy just to be here today, riding quietly through the countryside. Stopping on the bridge and looking down at the river, he looked around to make sure nobody was coming up behind him. Then, remembering the trout pool, he leaned over and looked down. There, just behind those rocks, he saw the gentle back swirl. A perfect safe place for a wise old trout to lurk. Possibly, if he was still on his feet once this was over, he'd dig up a few earthworms and see how smart that wily trout really was.

Coming into town he knew his first stop would be the general store. A man couldn't go without a hat. Dropping the reins across the hitch post in front of the false-fronted store, Buck held the door for a matronly woman carrying a cloth sack of groceries, and walked in. Standing just inside the door for a minute to let his eyes adjust to the gloom, he saw a tall, thin man behind the counter. Nodding, Buck asked about hats. Wordlessly the clerk pointed toward the back. Walking toward the back of the store, past the canned food section and tables piled high with men's pants and shirts, he spotted his goal. At the very back of the store, on shelves built against the back wall, were stacks of hats. Mostly Stetsons and mostly black, although some were a soft gray, but all with wide brims that would protect the wearer from any type of weather. Conscious of being watched by the clerk, he slowly went through the piles until he found one he thought he might like. It was a flat-topped black felt hat and when he gently set it on his head was pleased as it seemed to be a comfortable fit.

'I think this one will do just fine,' he said bringing his choice to the counter and reaching into a pocket for cash.

'Just got those unpacked this morning. The price for that one' — he said looking at the little tag tied to the thin brown leather hatband — 'is twelve dollars.'

Out on the boardwalk, Buck stopped and adjusted his new Stetson, all the while looking up and down the street. The hitching rail in front of the saloon was full with half-a-dozen horses standing hipshot and asleep. Strolling down the street he inspected the rumps and saw that all but one carried the H Bar H brand. Well, as someone had said, that wasn't surprising; the Hightowers sold a lot of good horses in this area. It is just possible that he'd be lucky and find both Hugh and Frank Hightower inside having a drink.

Buck stopped before pushing through the swinging doors and looked the place over. The long mahogany bar lined the left side of the long room with shelves of bottled goods against the wall. Tables, each with a scattering of chairs around them filled the rest of the space. The bartender, dirty white apron and round derby hat letting everyone know he was a professional, stood at the far end of the bar slowly drying a glass as he listened to one of the men on the other side of the barrier. Four or five men lined the bar on that side. Most of them, from their clothing, were towns-folk, only a couple wore typical range outfits of denim pants, high-heeled boots and gunbelts. One of the cowboys, the one doing the talking, was Frank Hightower.

Dusk had started darkening the sky while he was in the store buying his hat and the light was about the same as the smoky inside of the saloon. There was no need to let his eyes adjust so he placed both hands on the double doors and shoved. The noise of the doors swinging open caused the bartender to look up. More interested in whatever Frank was telling them, Buck only got a glance before the barkeep's attention shifted back to the speaker.

Settling his gunbelt comfortably on his hips, Armstrong took the few steps to the mahogany and leaned one elbow on the bar. 'Is that load of bull so entertaining that a man can't get a drink in here?' he asked loudly. Frank's voice stopped and the bartender jumped and started down to the new customer.

'By Gawd, you can just wait for your drink until I'm through talking, stranger.' Frank was drunk. Standing squarely he faced down the bar toward Buck.

'Stranger? Why Frank Hightower, I'm no stranger to you,' Buck challenged, causing Frank to take a closer look. Surprised, he paled and then yelled, 'Damn you. You're dead!'

27

'Well, not yet. I'm a very lively man looking for a coupla skunks, and you call me a stranger. Don't you remember holding me under the guns of you and your pa, tying me up and then beating me unconscious? I'm that stranger you and your pa then tied to my horse and took out into the sand blow and left with no water. Even taking my horse. Why, I had to come into town today just to replace the hat you didn't let me keep out there. Is that the tall tale you're telling these good people?'

'Don't think you can make any such claims. Not here. I'll have you know this is my town. You're nothing but a killer. It's because of you my little brother was shot. Damn you. You're nothing.' Frank's angry ranting made his face flush. Taking a step or two closer, he didn't notice the men who had been standing around him move away, out of the line of fire. The bartender had stopped and when Buck glanced his way, carefully placed both hands flat on the bar in front of him.

Frank's breath came in great gulps as he tried to speak over his rage. 'My pa is the head honcho of this basin. Once he gets control of that damn Randle woman's range he and I will be the power that everyone will have to deal with. And you think any of these people care about your little trip into the desert? They'd better only care about keeping the Hightowers happy. Damn.' He swung a fist against the bar in frustration, 'This wouldn't have happened if that stupid brother of mine had done what Pa told him and killed you before you even got here. Oh, you're lucky, I'll give you that. Pa had no trouble finding those rustlers. All he had to do is point out where they'd find a few bunches of cattle nobody was close to. Their greed took over from there until you butted in. We set up a stage robbery and who says you didn't do it? That dinky little snot Paul. He didn't even know enough to keep his mouth shut.' Without knowing it, with each statement he took a step or two closer and banged his fist on the wood.

'Yeah, you're lucky. Why you didn't die in the desert, I don't know. I tried to tell Pa that I should just go ahead and put you out of your misery, but oh, no, he wouldn't listen to me, would he? No. He had to get cute and run you out into the desert. So here you are, about to lose out after all. You can't stop us. How can you? We own this town. Don't you know the sheriff is ours? Hell, we even own the bank. You don't think that old fool Blount is smart enough for that, do you? Right now Pa is out at the widow's ranch, getting her to sign that place over. That's when things'll really happen. When we take over this valley, fools like you won't last an hour.'

Smiling through the man's haranguing, Buck reached up and carefully removed his new hat. Placing it squarely on the bar by his elbow, he turned to face the blustering horse breeder. Thumbing the thong from the hammer of his Colt, he chuckled.

'Frank, I think I'm going to give you a chance. Tell you what, we'll both unbuckle our gunbelts and go at it with our fists and boots. You'll lose, but I'm looking forward to paying you back for what you did while I was strung up. That's the only way someone like you can win a fight, having the other guy helpless. Well, come on, I'm not helpless now. Let's see what kind of man you really are.' He used one hand to slap the bar top and let the other drop causally to the butt of his .44.

'Damn you,' Frank swore, reaching for his Peacemaker. Those watching said later that Buck waited until Frank's gun cleared leather before pulling his own six-gun but nobody really saw his Colt Dragoon come up. One instant the pistol was in its holster and the next it was out and flame was shooting from the gun. Three shots were fired, Frank got his off first, but he'd been eager. His lead dug a hole in the floor as Buck's two shots, so close together they sounded like one, punched holes in Frank's chest, slamming his body back and against the bar. Dead on his feet, he slowly collapsed to end up sitting with his back against the bar. For a time nobody moved.

Watching the men, Buck waited to see how it would go. Finally, one man exhaled. 'Jesus. Did you hear all that? Damn.'

Nobody was looking at Buck, all were staring down at the dead man. Slowly, one at a time they glanced up at Buck and then at each other. The silence that covered the saloon like a blanket was broken when the doors were smashed open and Sheriff Holt came running in waving his double-barreled shotgun.

'What the hell is going on here?' he bellowed, slightly out of breath from his run down the street. Sliding to a stop when he saw Frank's body, he looked quickly up at Buck. Before he could raise the shotgun, Buck's Colt was pressed against the lawman's plump stomach. 'You! I might have known you'd be here, shooting up the place. Boy, you did it this time. That's one of the local rancher's sons you've killed this time. And before witnesses, too.'

'No, Sheriff. Those days are over. Frank was kind enough to explain just what he and his father, and you, were up to. Now, slowly hand that scattergun over to one of those men.' Startled, Holt did as he was told. The shopkeeper who reached out to take the shotgun didn't hesitate and looked the sheriff right in the eye.

'I'd say your time of wearing the badge is about over, Holt,' Buck shook his head. 'My advice is for you to leave that star on the bar and go find yourself a fast horse. I'm on my way down to the bank and after that I'll be riding out to the Rocking C. Don't be here when I come back through.'

Looking from face to face, the chubby man let his shoulders droop.

Unpinning his badge from his shirt he dropped it on to the bar and without another word, walked out dejectedly. Again nobody commented and the silence grew.

'Well, boys, looks like you'll have to find a new sheriff.' Buck replaced the spent shells in his Colt and looking around, smiled and walked out of the saloon.

28

Juan Navarro watched his son, hoping that once he had learned that the big cowboy hadn't been behind the shooting of his father he would return to his normal self. The old Basque snorted, normal self indeed. Once upon a time, back when Jose had been much younger and his mother was still alive, he had had hopes that the boy would grow straight, proud and tall. Not just in stature but in the terms of being a man. Somewhere, something had changed the once happy boy and made him a very serious young man. Juan wondered if not having a mother during all those years had caused this to happen.

Truly, there was little to complain about. Jose was very good with the sheep and the flocks, being healthy and well taken care of, had grown in size.

Since a very young boy, Jose had shown an instinct for knowing when and how far to move his flock each day. There was nothing more the older man could teach his son. It was not to do with the sheep that worried the father. There was something inside, something that caused Jose to brood that was the cause for his concern.

This morning, when the man, Armstrong, had joked about his appearance, Jose had found the humor and laughed. As the big black horse disappeared in the distance, he had gone about his work getting the sheep lined out to the little brown grass meadow he had been taking them this past few days. Soon, possibly even tonight, they would have to move the wagon and the flock on to a new area.

The sheep were fattening nicely for this time of year and the lamb crop had been good. When they moved south in preparation of making their fall shipment, Juan was sure it would turn out to be an excellent season. This year, feeling his years, he had decided not to travel with the loaded box cars but to let Jose handle that business on his own.

He had not said anything to the boy yet, of course. After being shot, Juan had taken things very easy, resting most of the day and not riding or walking out with the flock. Jose had not noticed, he believed, but the healing was slow going. The gash cut by the bullet had scabbed over and then mended leaving only a scar. A white mark on the outside, but sometimes, especially in the cool mornings, a red-hot streak of pain inside. This was something else he hid from his son. Sighing, he thought about all the things he was not sharing.

Juan was not surprised to find, when Jose returned to camp in the early evening, that the humor had gone from his eyes. With little conversation between the two men dinner was prepared and the dishes cleaned up. Settling back on his blanket with a full pipe burning smoothly and a mug of strong black tea, the old man decided it was time to make some of his thoughts known to his son. Jose, however, didn't pour his tea as usual. Standing by the fire for a few minutes, staring out into the coming darkness, he finally looked down at his father.

'There is something I must do, Father. Don't fret and do not wait up for me. I will return before first light.' In minutes he had saddled his horse and without another word, had ridden out of the camp. Juan Navarro listened until the silence of a night-time sheep camp returned. Customarily, after so many nights spent like this, the night sounds were comforting. Tonight, however, was different. Jose rode with one thought in mind. All day he had been thinking about the man, Armstrong. A strong man and, more than likely, a good man in his own world, but that was a separate world than the young sheepherder knew of. When he had found him lying face down in the rocky edges of the sand country, the thought

had been to just leave him and let
nature take its course. After all, this was
the man who had shot his father, wasn't
it? And even if it had been some other
cattleman, what did that matter? At
heart, they and their kind were all the
same.

But as he sat his saddle thinking
about it, he knew he couldn't just ride
away and leave him to die, if he wasn't
already dead. That would make him as
black-hearted as the man whose life he
now held in his hands.

Turning Armstrong's body over, he
saw that life was still there, barely.
Although painfully sunburned and bloody,
a soft groan and shallow breathing were
signs that the man still lived. After moist-
ening the wounded man's lips with a
wet cloth and wrapping the man's head
in a faded kerchief, he loaded him into
his own saddle and began the ride back
to the sheep camp. Riding slowly to
make the trip as smooth as possible,
Jose stopped every so often to wet the
unconscious man's mouth.

Back in camp, he had had to lift Armstrong off his horse and then, with his father's help, gently cleaned the dried blood from the cuts. It took hours of applying wet cloths to his lips and face before the near-dead man's breathing became stronger. Sleep was the great healer and, although at times restless, he slept through most of the night and the entire next day.

Jose and his father had worked to save the man's life even though he might have been the one who had shot the older sheepherder. When Armstrong had made his argument, proving to Jose that it had been some other rancher, the young man had felt relief. That is until he thought it all over while with the flock the next day. It wasn't enough to have worked to save the big man, he decided. There was still evil out in the world. Now he was riding toward that evil.

The young sheepman wasn't exactly sure where he would find his quarry, but thought a good place to start would be at the Rocking C. Mr and Mrs Randle had always been friendly to the Basque sheepherders, and anyway, he couldn't think of where else to start. Perhaps he would end up crossing the river and riding to the horse-breeder's ranch, but he'd never been there and didn't like the idea of wandering around blindly.

It wasn't that Jose thought of himself as a brave man, or a coward either for that matter. He had never shot anyone before and didn't know if he'd be able to do it. A flush of shame passed over his face as he thought about taking the old Winchester out of the wagon. He hoped his father hadn't noticed the barrel sticking out of the bedroll tied to his saddle. Somehow, he felt that hiding the weapon was almost like stealing. Riding armed into the enemy camp, though, was not something that he wanted to do if he didn't have to.

An ambush on the trail? Jose shook the thought away. Too much like what the real killer had done to his father. He'd just have to wait and see.

29

'Matilda, I'm making this my last offer,' Hightower said coldly. He had ridden into the Rocking C ranch at dusk and without so much as a hello, tied his horse to the rail and stormed into the house. Matilda, hearing the horse coming into the yard, had smiled, thinking it was Buck returning for something. When the front door slammed open, she frowned and put down the coffee pot of water she had just poured, and hastened out of the kitchen, coming to an abrupt halt when she saw who it was.

'Damn it, woman. This is not easy for me, but I can't be put off any longer. Will you agree to marry me so I can take care of you or not? I want to know what your mind is.' Hugh wasn't yelling, but he was hard and demanding. Matilda was nearly speechless.

Finally, seeing the blackness behind the man's eyes, she started shaking her head in denial. 'No, Hugh. I won't be bullied into marrying you or anyone. Who do you think you are, anyway, bursting in here and making demands? Are you drunk? Go home and sleep it off. Go on' — the more she talked the madder she became — 'get out of my house.'

Hightower rocked back on his heels. A thin smile brought his lips into a slight curve. 'I guess you've made it clear. Too bad, but just like any female it won't do any good trying to change your mind.' Taking a quick step forward, he grabbed her arm and twisting it around, forced her hand up behind her back. Matilda was too surprised to do anything but whimper at the sudden pain.

Pushing against her arm, he almost ran her ahead of him back into the kitchen. Slamming her down into one of the wood chairs at the big table he took a pigging string from a pocket and quickly tied her hands to the chair arms. Moaning with shock over the sudden harsh treatment, Matilda wilted.

Laughing at the sight of the young woman now helpless, Hugh casually finished the job of making the pot of coffee. Pouring a handful of crushed coffee beans into the pot of water, he stoked up the fire in the stove's firebox and placed the pot on the hot top.

'Now, let's have a cup of fresh coffee and talk about what's the best thing for you to do,' he said pleasantly. 'That's all I've wanted, you know, is what's best for you. Why do you think I offered to marry you? It would have made everything much easier. But no, you had to think you knew what's best. Well, it doesn't matter. In the end, it won't matter at all. I will get what I want and everything will come out just the same.'

As the coffee pot started to boil, Hugh, settling his gunbelt more comfortably on his waist, leaned one hip on the counter and watched the woman.

Jerking against the thongs that held her, she quickly realized her helplessness. Unable to move, she sat for a minute or two and then, flipping her head up to swing her hair out of her eyes she glared at her captor.

'What are you talking about? You couldn't be serious about my marrying you. My Virgil hasn't even been in the ground but a short time; how could you think I've given any thought about marrying anyone?' Slowly, as her early scare faded, some inner strength developed.

'That's what I tried to tell you. A woman just doesn't understand enough about things to be successful when it comes to running a spread like this. Why, I'll bet you've never given any notion to what it means to be the biggest rancher in the valley. Your precious Virgil didn't, that's for sure. He was too easily satisfied. He could've been the most powerful man in this part of the state, but I doubt he was smart enough to see it. Well, his loss is going to be my gain.'

'Hugh Hightower, I think there is something wrong with you. Now, cut me loose and we'll have a cup of coffee and forget all about this.'

That brought another chuckle from the man. Turning to move the boiling coffee pot off the hot stove, he shook his head. 'You're just a woman, how could I expect you to see beyond the kitchen?' he asked. 'Take that mess you helped make of my youngest boy Paul. It's just something a woman would do, turn a spineless boy against his family by throwing some dirt clod piece of girl at him. That made me very angry and sooner or later those people will pay for it. But first there's the little business of you to take care of. I found out a long time ago, there're easy ways to tame a horse and there are hard ways. At the end of the day, though, the horse does what I want.'

Matilda pulled against the ties binding her arms to the chair. 'That sounds like you, thinking you can tame people just like you would a horse. It doesn't work like that, Hugh. People aren't dumb animals.'

'Oh, horses aren't dumb. Why, I could name a lot of people who are a sight dumber.'

'Someone like Buck Armstrong?' she asked, and almost flinched at the sudden fury that covered his face.

'Armstrong,' he snarled, and then, relaxing, looked at her with scorn. 'That's one man I was very happy to get rid of. You don't have to look for him to help you any more. By now he's nothing more than a sunburned crisp.'

'Oh? Then you don't know.'

'Know what? He's gone, I tell you. His horse was found out near the sand blow. That fool probably got lost and wasn't carrying enough water,' Relaxed, he poured a cup of coffee and, blowing at the steam, sat down at the table across from Matilda. 'Anyway, he's gone. Take my word for it, he's dead.'

'Just this afternoon he was sitting just

where you are. I cooked him a nice steak for lunch. He looked like he'd been out in the sun too long, but he was his usual self.'

'No. That couldn't be,' Hightower snapped, then once again calmed himself down. 'But that doesn't matter. Not now and not to you. What matters to you is that you're tied to that chair. And there's nobody to come to rescue you. So, here's what I want from you: A signed paper telling everyone how you decided to sell this place to me. Say you can't stand to be here anymore. You write that out like I say and I'll set you free.'

'I don't understand you, Hugh. Nobody would believe I'd do such a thing.'

'No, it's you who don't understand. Once I'm in control of the Rocking C there's nobody that'll go against me. I've been planning this since your pa died. With this spread joined to mine I'll be the biggest man in the area. Look, so far my plans have been good. I fixed it with Hubbard to hold those IOUs. Those and the bogus bank-loan papers should have been enough for you to simply do as I wanted. But no, that damn Armstrong had to show up.'

'What do you mean, bogus loan papers?'

'Your dear husband didn't gamble, although I certainly tried to get him into a few games. But he did like to drink. That was when I decided it didn't matter, I'd simply sign his name on the pieces of paper and when the gambler made his claim, everybody thought they were real.'

'But I saw them, they had Virgil's signature on them.'

'No, that's another thing that old Blount is good at, copying people's signatures. It even fooled you, didn't it?'

'Blount? Why would he be involved with you?'

'Because I own the bank and he works for me. I told you, I've been planning this for a long time.' Finishing his cup of coffee, he stood up and put the empty cup in the dry sink. 'Now see, if you were smarter you'd realize that I don't need your signature on a piece of paper. Blount can do it for me. Hell, I don't need you at all. Fact is' — he frowned in thought — 'it'd probably be better if you simply disappeared.' He thought for a minute and then smiled. 'No, better if you had an accident. Yes, people would be more likely to understand if you signed the place over to me and then, poor woman, got caught in a fire.'

'Hugh, you're crazy. You'd never get away with something like that.'

'Sure I would.' Looking around the homely kitchen he grinned, 'It's too bad, though. This is a nice place. Ah, well. Frank and the boys wouldn't understand how to live in some place like this. They're more used to a bunkhouse or the barn. Come on, let's get on with it.' Saying that, he walked around behind her and taking hold of the chair leaned it back and dragged her, chair and all, out into the short hall.

'That's the best place. The pigging strings will burn off and there'll be no sign that you didn't just get caught in the blaze.'

30

Night had fallen and full darkness covered Jose's arrival at the Randle ranch house. Seeing a horse tied to the porch rail, he reined behind a corral and rode slowly and quietly behind the barn. Quickly securing his mount and taking the rifle, he stole around the corner, stopping where he could see the front of the house.

The near full moon was high enough to cast its weak yellowing light on the house and yard. From the shadows, Jose watched the house and tried to think of what to do next. Lantern light defused by curtains outlined a back window, probably a kitchen window, he figured. He had just about decided to cross over to the house and try to see into that window when a man came out of the front door.

Instinctively, Jose backed deeper in

the shadow when the man, slamming the door behind him, came striding across to the barn. Scarcely breathing he waited as the man stalked by, passing within ten feet of his hidden rifle. The man, not looking right or left, went out of sight. Jose listened, jumping when he heard a door being yanked open.

Sounds of the man cursing as he broke one match after another, until one fired and light spread as a lantern was lit. Looking through a crack between two wall boards, Jose saw that the man was Hightower, the man he'd come to find.

Sweat broke out on the young man's face. Here he was and all he had to do was lift the rifle and point it. Pulling the trigger would be just what the horse breeder had done to his father. Jose, watching Hightower walk quickly along one wall and then enter what was obviously a tack-room, waited. He couldn't just shoot the man in the back.

Wiping his hands one at a time on

his pants, Jose continued watching, one eye to the crack. Laughing, Hightower came out of the tack-room and holding the lantern in one hand and a tin container in the other, stomped out of the barn. Jose was frozen with fear as the rancher went by. Setting the lantern on the ground in front of the porch, Hightower twisted the cap off the can and started pouring liquid along the wall. The smell of coal oil filled the air and told Jose what he was planning.

Eventually tossing the now empty container aside, Hightower picked up the lantern and threw it against the wall. Instantly the fire raced up the wood. Standing back a few feet, Hightower put his hands on his hips and laughed.

Shocked, Jose stepped out of the dark and, bringing the rifle to his shoulder, yelled, 'Hightower! Turn around.'

'What?' Hightower turned quickly, reaching for his handgun as he came around. Hesitating an instant while he tried to see who had called, he was bringing the revolver's barrel up when Jose fired. Not waiting to see where his first shot had gone, Jose quickly levered another shell into the chamber and shot again. The first shot had taken Hightower in the upper chest, throwing him back. Off balance, his body tried to stay upright when the second bullet, glancing off the big belt buckle, tore up under his rib cage. Like a rag doll, the man folded.

The night was suddenly filled with sound as a big black horse came charging into the yard. Frightened by what he had done, Jose slipped back around the barn and jumped into the saddle. Racing away, he only glanced back after reaching the safety of darkness. The glow didn't seem to be getting any bigger. Slapping the reins against his horse's neck, Jose was surprised to discover he was sobbing.

31

Earlier, just shy of full darkness, Buck found the bank's door had been locked and shades pulled down over the windows. Shadows cast on the shades by the lantern light somewhere inside told him that at least one person was still inside, though. Knocking loudly on the door, he waited.

'Go away,' a man yelled from inside. 'We're closed. Come back in the morning.'

He pounded his fist against the door again, and once more was told to go away. A third hammering and the shade blocking the full length windows of the door was pulled aside. Buck didn't recognize the face frowning at him. Shaking his head, the unknown man once more ordered Buck to go away. Drawing his pistol, the big man pointed it and smiled. Glancing behind him, the thin-faced man swung quickly around when Buck tapped the glass with the gun barrel.

'Open the door or I'll have to start breaking glass,' he warned. Quickly taking a large key from his pants pocket, the door was unlocked. Reaching one hand to the door knob, Buck pushed the door open forcing the man inside to almost lose his balance.

'Who are you?' he asked, tapping the man on his thin bony chest. Everything about the man was thin, from his nearly bald head to his patent leather shoes.

Nervously the man gulped and stammered, 'Henry. I'm the teller. Mr Blount is back in his office. Is this a hold-up?'

'Nope. Just want to have a little talk with the banker. You just sit over there,' he motioned with his gun, 'and don't move. OK?'

'Yes, sir,' and he sat down meekly on the edge of the leather-covered seat.

Buck smiled and walked to the office door and pushed it open.

'God damn it, Henry — ' Blount growled, stopping when he looked up and into the dark end of the Colt's barrel. 'What,' he stammered, never taking his eyes off that black tunnel. 'What do you want?' Finally looking up, his face blanched as he recognized the man holding the gun. 'You . . . you're dead.'

'Nope, you're the second one to make that mistake tonight. The first, Frank Hightower, is, though. I wouldn't make the same mistake he did and try reaching into that drawer.' Blount's hand had been moving, but at Buck's words jerked back as if snake bit.

'Things have been changing, while you were closing up, Mr Blount. Sheriff Holt has left town, or is trying to as fast as he can. The last time I saw young Hightower he was lying on the floor of the saloon with a coupla holes in him. And soon I'll be out looking for the elder Hightower. I guess that means it's your turn.' Buck hitched one hip on the side of the big wood desk.

'What do you mean?' Blount's face had turned pale but flushed as he saw Buck relax.

'Well, from what Frank said before I shot him, you seem to have been part of his pa's plans for becoming the big bull of the woods. Yes,' he went on, as the banker shook his head, 'he had been drinking which led to bragging, which led to his making his last mistake. And all those townsfolk enjoying his brag heard how you don't own the bank, Hightower does. I guess if you stay in town, you're going to be getting a lot of grief. But then, once Hugh Hightower is gone, what with his two boys having been killed, I'd say that puts the bank in Paul's hands. Somehow I don't think young Paul will like what he hears about you. The best thing is for you to follow Holt. Get a fast horse or, if you're brave, wait for the morning stage and get out of town. Fact is, you had better be long gone when I come back through town a little later.'

'But I can't just walk away. I've put a

lot of work in making this bank profitable. You can't expect me to just ride out and leave it. Be reasonable.'

'Oh, but I am reasonable. You're getting the chance to ride out without any extra holes in your measly hide. Now, where are the keys to that big black safe?'

'Here, in my pocket.'

'OK, be very careful and drop them on the desk.' Looking at the firearm once more pointing at his nose, Blount obeyed quickly. Standing, Buck used the six-gun to direct Blount to get up.

'Hey, Henry,' Buck called, as he drove the banker out of his office by poking him in the back. 'Did you hear all that? Good. Then listen to this. Do you have a revolver back there?' At a nod, he smiled. 'Better. Now, old Blount here is going to walk out and never come back. If he tries to, you get that weapon and shoot him. If you don't and he takes one dollar out of here, I'll shoot you. And that would make our friendly banker a thief and I'd go looking for him and shoot him myself. Am I being clear?' Quickly both men nodded in agreement.

'Fine. Good night, Henry. Blount, get running before I change my mind.'

★ ★ ★

Riding out to the Rocking C, Buck wasn't in any great hurry until coming close to the ranch yard, he saw a sudden glow near where the house sat. At the same time he heard two shots fired. Knocking his boot heels against the sides of the black stallion, he raced into the ranch yard.

A body was sprawled out on the ground, but he didn't stop to see who it was. His full attention was on the blaze running along the side wall. Jumping out of the saddle, he ran to the water trough and, seeing a bucket, filled it and started fighting the fire. The smell of coal oil was strong, but apparently most of it had been poured on the ground, missing the structure. Within a few minutes, and no more than a dozen buckets from the trough, the fire had been put out. The last bucket Buck poured over his head.

Resting against the side of the house, Armstrong took a long look at the man's body lying a few yards away. Hugh Hightower. Turning the body over on its back, he saw what the bullets had done. The only person he could think of who could have done the shooting was Matilda, but if that was the case, where was she? Faintly he heard someone calling.

With his Colt ready, Buck pushed open the front door with the toe of a boot. 'Help me . . . damn it, come help me.' Matilda's yells came out of the dark interior.

'Matilda? Are you all right?'

'Buck? Is that you? Watch out, Hugh's around somewhere. I think he's gone crazy.'

Moving across the living-room Buck smiled when he found her lying on her side, still tied to the chair. 'Now why are you just lying there? Don't tell me you missed out on all the excitement.'

'Excitement? What was the shooting? And where's Hugh?'

'Did he do this to you?' he asked, as he set the chair upright and quickly cut her loose. 'Hugh is beyond doing more harm. He's out in the yard. Someone put two big holes in his chest. Fact is, that just about takes all the fight out of the Hightower family. Paul's the only one left.'

Quickly he explained what he had been doing in town, and after throwing a tarp over Hightower's body and again inspecting the scorched wall, they returned to the kitchen. The pot of coffee Hugh had made was still hot and while they calmed down with a cup, she told him all that Hugh had done and said.

'Matilda, back when the Professor's letter came, telling you that I was going to stop by, was there anyone who knew about it?'

'No, well, I guess Hugh knew. He

brought my mail out that time and I was pretty excited about Uncle Fish sending someone to help me. Things were pretty dark and dismal then, and Hugh was just starting to talk about helping me. Why?'

'According to something that Frank said, one of the men who tried to ambush me when I was coming into the valley was his brother Hughie. I don't know who the third man was. Guess I never will, now.'

'Everything that was happening then, was Hugh's doings? He had always been a friend and neighbor; it's hard to believe.'

'Well, maybe not everything. I'll go lay him out in the barn for tonight. We'll have to somehow get hold of Paul tomorrow and let him know what has happened.'

Later, after unsaddling his horse and turning it out into one of the corrals, he carried Hightower's body into the barn and covered the remains again with the tarp. Using the lantern, he found

Hightower's revolver. It was an old model Colt. A .36 caliber five-shot revolver, the kind Buck hadn't seen too many of in his travels. Most all of those he had seen had been refitted from black powder to take cartridges. Hugh's weapon hadn't been converted. Holding the heavy firearm he thought about the long octagonal-barreled pistol. Shooting black powder, if the target was anywhere within a yard or two, the chances were good it would leave a smoke-blackened wound. Without a confession, this was pretty convincing proof that both Virgil and Hubbard had been killed with this gun.

Matilda had argued when he said he'd drop his bedroll in one of the stalls. There were very good beds in the house and no reason for him not to take advantage of one. Giving her one of his smiles, he agreed. Now, with the tarp-covered body up off the dirt floor on a wide plank, he walked down to one of the hay-filled stalls and unrolled his bedding.

32

Early the next morning, after washing up in the water trough, he was on his way back to the barn to saddle up when he spotted a couple of shell casings lying in the dirt near a corner of the barn. Picking one up, he noticed a slight oily feel. Sniffing his fingers brought back the memory of the salve Juan had used on his sunburn. A salve made from a sheep's oily wool. Looking out toward the far horizon, he nodded, before tossing the shells into a nearby scrap heap.

Breakfast was heavy thick slices of bacon with eggs fried in the bacon grease. Freshly made baking-powder biscuits and lots of homemade butter filled whatever parts of his stomach were left over. Matilda didn't comment on his failure to return to the house the night before, but it wasn't until the second cup of coffee that Buck could relax.

The sound of horses coming into the yard took both out to the porch in time to see Paul and Elizabeth ride in. Both were on fine-looking H Bar H horses. Sitting on the porch, Buck and Matilda took turns telling the couple what had happened to the Hightower family. Without saying anything, Paul got up and walked to the barn, while the other three went back into the house.

Later, over lunch, Paul asked Buck what he thought he should do, now that he was the owner of a ranch and the town's bank.

'You're asking the wrong person, Paul. I'm just a hard riding cattleman without a single head of stock. Why, if you ask half the people around here they'll tell you I'm some kinda killer. Now, Matilda here has a good head on her shoulders, a pretty one too. I'm sure between the three of you, someone can be found to help you make as few mistakes as possible.'

Finishing his coffee, he stood and picked up his new hat. 'Meanwhile, I've got some business in town to finish up.'

Stepping into the saddle, he took up the reins and looked down as Matilda put her hand on his leg.

'Buck.' She looked up, letting her soft pale-blue eyes speak wordlessly. 'You know there's a place for you here. Old Hugh might have been right, I can't run this place by myself. You don't have to go, do you?'

For a minute he looked deeply in her eyes and then reaching up with his hand, touched his hat brim. 'Matilda, I'm not the kind of fellow to hang around working at ranching. If I stayed, the time would come when one morning I wouldn't be there. Naw, all it would take is a letter from the professor and I'd be up on this mean old stud horse and gone. You're going to have good neighbors; the farmers are good people and those Basque sheepherders are real special. You'll be all right.'

Smiling, he gigged the horse and

reined away riding out of the ranch yard. Down the road, he turned and gave a big wave before touching the horse into a trot.

THE END